The Witch & the Wanderer

Volume 1

By Ben. Townsend

Contents

To everyone who ever encouraged me. Small acts of kindness truly do go a long way.

Prologue

With each passing day, the sun will once again rise in the east and set in the west. An endless cycle that routinely abandons the inhabitants of the world, leaving them to be subjected to hours of a cripplingly dark night, during which time most folk can do little more than pray for safe sleep. This reality of nature exists in the set of things about life that can simply never change. But people's perception of these things, though, is something that can be changed as effortlessly as the clothes they wear.

The dark forests of the night are home to limitless things that can ominously creak, hiss, or howl beneath the shroud that envelopes them. In ages past, children used to sit around fires at night, and be told stories of witches, monsters, and other wicked things that dabbled with evil magic in the shadows, looking to curse and condemn anyone who happened to be unsuspecting enough of their presence. Children and adults alike are afraid of things they can neither see nor understand, but it was this fear that kept them behind thick walls at night; that kept them safe.

In the times of late though, people are no longer raised to believe such eerie and mystical ideas. Children are only taught to fear wolves, disease, or strangers. The very concept of anything that can be considered supernatural has fallen into obscurity. They are mere tales of legends of myths that are disregarded and forgotten just as easily as the face of a random passerby on the streets. Still though, there are a few who covet the old tales, if only due to the *idea that believing in their mysteriousness makes life just that much more interesting.*

Because the truth is that anything could be hiding within the darkness of the world, and until confronted, its nature will forever be just as unknown as whether or not it even exists.

Chapter One

Rebirth

Horse hooves and cheap leather boots stepped and clacked around and about as the early afternoon market traffic reached its bustling peak. Hundreds of people stood around a large and open town square, haggling with vendors, shimmying through their pockets and coin purses, and muttering vulgar profanity at the many clearly inflated prices.

Apart from all the noisy and packed together crowds though, was Ronin, a young and light brown-haired boy who sat nestled up in the tight and lonesome crevices of a nearby back alleyway. His face was masked from any who glanced in his direction by a tattered, hole infested gray cloak that reeked of dried-up muck. He hunched over in his seat in contemplation, letting the sounds of the busy world around him pass by with the same lack of care that the folk who caused them held for him. This was perhaps the tenth, or possibly eleventh city or town he'd visited in the last few months. Ronin had lost count some time ago, and was not even completely sure of the name of the place he was currently residing in.

Presently, he had spent the entirety of the day, as well as each day prior, traveling the continent somewhat aimlessly, and approaching each and every innkeeper, librarian, scholar, and priest he could find, in the hopes that they could shed some light on a mystery. A mystery that had long since lingered in the back of his mind, pinching and prodding at his feigned apathy for all his years, until one day, he just couldn't take it anymore.

Ronin carried a small handcloth. Despite its clear age showing, the cloth was quite decorative and ornate, and far more luxurious looking than any of the glorified rags he was adorned in, as well as the few personal possessions he had to his name. Over the years his mind had been kissed by the temptation to try and pawn it off to some quirky shopkeeper more times than he could count, but the value of this cloth was something that even the shiniest chunks of gold could not equate to. Sewn into the bottom corner of it, was a crest. A lone black raven perched within the decorative shield turned its head towards the leftmost edge of the fabric, eternally staring off into the distance at something unknown.

It was a crest from his home and his family, whom he had never met, heard from, nor even heard about. And apparently, not a single intellectual in the entire Kingdom of Rendolyn seemed to have heard of them either.

Ronin held the cloth with both hands, and spread it out in front of his lowered gaze. Over the years he'd carefully examined every individual thread of the cloth. The fabric was made from the finest silk, and despite having weathered who knows how many years, it remained impeccably smooth. Such a commodity could only be acquired in relatively small amounts via strenuous and expensive imports from far eastern lands. The fact that a family could afford to have their crest custom embedded into something as insignificant as a stupid hand cloth undoubtedly meant that wealth was as plentiful to them as grains of sand were to a beach.

"And they couldn't even leave me with bread money..." Ronin begrudgingly thought to himself.

Aside from this, he'd long since run out of thoughts about the cloth. For the millionth time, he followed the raven's gaze leftwards. Ten or so feet ahead, he saw a wrinkled tarp loosely tied over a damaged wall breezing in the wind. A second later, the weak fabric tore from its knots and fluttered away, vanishing around a corner. Ronin let out a deep groan of frustration before not so gently jamming the cloth back into his bag. He'd never felt so helpless before in his life. He leaned back to rest against the cold wall behind him. In spite of his discouragement, there was a slight sense of comfort and familiarity Ronin found in claustrophobic alleys like this one, regardless of the danger they sometimes posed. He rested his eyes, and pulled his hood down over his face to get some more shade from the daylight. Even though the day was still bright and young, a part of him simply wanted it to be over.

He was eventually roused by the deep voiced shouting of one of the town guards who had taken notice of his admittedly sketchy appearance.

"For the lord's sake I can't believe my eyes. To think that damnable smugglers have been making off with our market's goods day after day for ages now, and a sludge-stained rascal like yourself can still possess the audacity to linger around in the shadows," called out the tall and hulking man as he stomped his way over. He arrived swiftly, only to incessantly bark about town standards and safety for the common folk in an obviously power tripping speech, before ordering Ronin to empty his pockets so that he could check for any potentially stolen goods. Ronin slowly rose to his feet, and stared back at the guard.

"How typical," he thought, but remained behaved nonetheless. This man was a complete caricature in Ronin's eyes; an overly dramatic yapper with the stench of cheap ale laced into his breath, and who probably had a few buddies or a tavern lass watching from the crowd of nearby people the confrontation had drawn the attention of. He of course voiced none of these assumptions though, and instead simply raised his arms and allowed himself to be searched.

"Grr... " groaned the clearly annoyed guard when he found basically nothing of value on Ronin aside from a few cheap coins and an expectedly unrecognizable crest on the handcloth. He spat to the ground, and threw the open cloth down before shoving Ronin away and leaving. With a shake of his head, Ronin crouched to retrieve his possession, then turned to walk further into the alley.

The back-end pits of most of the towns and cities he ventured to were all pretty much indistinguishable from one another. Gutters leaked old filthy water into dark puddles littered across the ground, as rats and other stray animals darted and dashed between the shadows, looking to scavenge whatever scraps they could find.

Ronin paused briefly when he caught sight of one of the smaller rats carefully watching him from beneath an old box. He smiled weakly at it before fishing some leftover crumbs out of his pocket and tossing them towards the little thing.

"Make sure to share," he said with far more empathy than most humans cared to have for such irrelevant creatures. Somehow, he considered them to be better company that most of the people whom he passed by on the streets. This was probably because such critters could hardly be blamed for the myriad of shattered windows and collapsing rooftops that infested these places alongside them. Poverty was very much a man-made state of existence in Ronin's eyes, and one that seemingly all folk would flee from as if it were the plague, but not hesitate to cast others into, especially if it fueled their own route.

Ronin had a strong instinct for navigating these maze-like alleyways after having spent so much time in them. He continued to squeeze his way through, searching for a pleasantly isolated path to one of the city's gates so that he could continue his journey elsewhere before nightfall.

After a few more twists and turns, he arrived in a small square clearing between a few old buildings. The wall around the city was in sight just ahead, so finding one of the exits would be as simple as following the perimeter of the barrier until he arrived. He moved forward towards another tight corridor, but just as he was about to step through, a strange and disturbing figure emerged from around a corner to block his path.

He was a tall and imposing man, who like Ronin, concealed much of his person beneath a long-hooded cloak, only his was of far greater quality. Its dark green material wrapped itself around the man like a stage curtain, with who knew what hiding behind it. Part of his face was also concealed by his apparel, but several deep scars were still visibly gashed into the aged skin of his cheeks. He glared silently at Ronin for a longish moment, refusing to blink as he seemingly examined every inch of the younger boy's appearance, until he sighed in a way that sounded suspiciously relieved.

"Guards never act with any subtlety, that's how you know they're only in their line of work for the superficial respect and attention, am I right?" he asked at last with a raspy voice, but didn't give Ronin time to respond. "On a better day I'd offer more pleasantries, but I'm afraid I'm far too pressed for time and opportunity at the moment. You're coming with me. Toss all of your belongings over then turn around and hold your hands behind your back."

Ronin carefully made sure to display no emotion as he matched this man's threatening gaze. This stranger was far from the first person who'd ever tried to corner him in an alley, so Ronin knew that any visible sign of weakness would be pounced on immediately. Still though, he couldn't help but feel intimidated by the man's professional attire and demeanor. He was certainly no common crook.

"Who are you?" asked Ronin, but the man replied with nothing other than an assertive step forward. In response, Ronin cautiously took a step back, only to have his worst fears confirmed in full when the man without hesitation swung his cloak around his back to reveal an assortment of deadly weapons that included a shining steel dagger, the sharpness of which was certainly enough to make a wolf's fangs jealous.

"I know what you're thinking, and trust me, you don't stand a chance," said the man without the slightest hint of doubt in his voice. Ironically, if the man had exclusively wanted to just steal all of his things, then Ronin felt that he honestly might have complied. However, being abducted into whatever slave ring or other inhumane atrocity this person could possibly be a part of was certainly not the most appealing direction he could fathom his life going.

"Alright," Ronin said fearfully as he finally allowed himself to tremble. However, this was just to feign submission as he slowly reached to his side to grab his bag, only to suddenly kick around and begin sprinting off back into the maze of alleys that surrounded them.

Running was perhaps the one thing that a wandering rascal like Ronin was indisputably gifted at. He first ran in a straight line to gain distance on his foe, but then started to zig zag his way through the terrain to break line of sight. As he dashed throughout the various paths, he made sure to toss down crates, barrels, and other debris behind himself in an effort to slow down his pursuer, while also keeping a careful eye out for any especially narrow routes that only his considerably skinnier figure would be able to fit through.

The rush of the situation kicked in quickly for Ronin, who for a moment felt a surge of confidence from his experienced tactics and maneuvers. This sensation did not last for long though, as the sounds of heavy boots stampeding their way towards him roared louder and louder with each passing second. Ronin took a split second look over his shoulder, but regretted it immediately as he witnessed the man a mere ten or so feet behind him, and rapidly closing the distance. Ronin quickly spun himself around the nearest corner, barely avoiding the man's lunging grasp as their chase continued. He may have been an excellent runner, but it was clear that this mysterious figure was an equally skilled chaser.

"I just have to make it back to the market..." Ronin thought to himself. From there, he could either hope that some guards would interrupt the situation, or at the very

least he could try to lose the man in the crowd. He ran as fast as his throbbing heart and weary legs would allow, but strangely, he no longer heard the man following him from behind. Soon enough, he turned another corner to see a large crowd of people not too far in the distance. He started running towards them, but made it no more than a few steps before stopping as he saw that the man had somehow managed to outmaneuver him, as he appeared in the middle of the path to cut off Ronin's escape.

An audible gasp served as the first true instance of Ronin's emotions betraying his otherwise wholly stoic persona. He could feel streams of sweat trickling down his shivering skin as in the span of less than a second, he struggled to imagine why anyone so menacing would ever bother to put in this much effort to try and capture someone as unremarkable as he was. He turned back around and sprinted further into the alleys, his pursuer hot on his trail once again.

Ronin fled for some time longer until he eventually found himself in view of the city's outer wall again. There was little else besides open space branching off to his left and right, and he began to wheeze loudly as he felt his malnourished body slowly start to succumb to exhaustion. He knew he didn't have the stamina to run forever, and as he approached the base of the wall, he instead decided to take a desperate jump as high as he could towards it. He latched his fingers and feet onto whatever cracks within the wood and stone of the structure that he could find. His grip was poor, and he could feel the old planks he clung to so tightly stab splinters into his hands. His entire body suddenly felt immensely heavier, as if an anvil had been strapped to his waist, but nevertheless he forced himself to climb and soon heaved himself to the top of the wall. He then proceeded to carefully drop down into the fields outside the city before making his way the forest in the distance.

Ronin didn't dare allow himself to feel even a cautious sense of relief though, as he knew his success would be short-lived. The man after him would obviously be able to perform such a feat himself, whoever he was. When Ronin arrived at the tree line, the terrain of the entire landscape started to slope upwards in a wide hill. He had no choice but to progress forward, much to the miserable strain of his muscles and lungs. Ronin trampled over leaves and stones, and shoved aside branches and bushes as he forced his way deeper into the woods.

He was soon stopped dead in his tracks though as he abruptly came to the dreadful realization that the particular direction he'd gone led to nowhere other than the edge of a roughly thirty foot high rocky cliff. He shot his gaze left, right, down, and even up as he futilely searched for any possible escape route, until he winced remorsefully and accepted that he had nowhere left to go.

Sure enough, he could once again hear his pursuer not far behind, but soon the footsteps were eerily reduced to silence. With a one last fearful gulp, Ronin managed to ease his shakiness as much as he could hope for before turning to face the man so committed to hunting him down. The man stood about ten feet ahead, and had his hood lowered to reveal his ruffled gray hair, as well as more scars that seemed to slither down past his neck.

"You're certainly worth more than you look; that was the longest I've had to run for in a while," he said with a modicum of respect. The man huffed in between his sentences, clearly feeling somewhat winded himself.

"Look, if this is about something I stole, then I'll gladly work to pay you or whomever you work for back. If you just give me a day or two to scout out the city, I promise I can get you something far more valuable," said Ronin in an effort to negotiate. He lowered his own hood as well, hoping the desperate expression on his face would make his offer seem a lot more sincere than it actually was. The man ignored his pleas for the moment though.

"You're practically still a kid... " he said, sounding a little regretful.

"Just seventeen winters, and I've been alone with no place to stay for many of them. I'm nobody, and you're obviously somebody. So why am I important to you?" Ronin demanded to know. The man shook his head and sighed.

"No deals, no questions. Please, don't make this any more difficult than you already have," he said while drawing a pair of binds from his belt. The man paused for a short second, then broke into an abrupt sprint straight towards Ronin. Ronin stood firmly as if to brace himself against the charge, but at last second attempted to nimbly dodge beneath the man's outstretched arms. Ronin was too slow though, and quickly found himself tackled to the ground in a losing wrestling bout.

He squirmed to try and free himself as the man tried to force Ronin's struggling hands into the bindings. The feeble strength of Ronin's scrawny arms was no challenge for his much older and bigger foe. As he realized how hopeless it would be for him to try and directly overpower the man, Ronin instead retaliated by curling his head inwards towards his own chest, before swiftly shooting it back in the other direction, causing the top of his head to harshly collide against the taller man's jaw.

The man grunted painfully as he was struck, and was left momentarily stunned. He reflexively loosened his grip on Ronin's wrists, giving the younger boy just enough time to reach down and grab the steel dagger he'd seen earlier, and plunge it through a slit in the man's armor, straight into his side. The man shrieked in pain as the deadly sharp weapon pierced into his flesh with ease. He grabbed Ronin by the shoulders and attempted to push away from him, but Ronin wrapped an arm around the man's neck and clung to him tightly while twisting the blade from side to side. Out of desperation, the man quickly drew a small concealed blade from inside his sleeve, and stabbed Ronin right back in his own side. Crows could be heard fleeing from the trees as the two of them wailed more and more. Ronin was forced to release his hold on the man, who promptly leapt backwards as the two of them slowly stumbled to their feet.

The man groaned in pain, but drew another blade from his sleeve as he weakly attempted to charge Ronin again, but made it no further than a single step before collapsing down. Ronin waited a few seconds to see if the man would get up, but he remained unresponsive on the ground. Ronin groaned in horrendous pain, and with one hand pressed firmly against his open wound, he slugged around in circles aimlessly, feeling weaker with each passing second.

As the thought of death appeared in his mind with absolute sincerity for the first time in his life, Ronin found himself suddenly praying to numerous deities from a multitude of old faiths that he didn't even believe in. His heart winced with almost as much pain as his side as he considered that the only person in the world who would potentially care, or even simply know about his untimely death, would be the very man responsible for it, and that such knowledge would still die with the both of them anyways.

Ronin felt his legs go weak as blood continued to drip down his side. In a last-ditch effort, he slowly started to trudge away, when all of a sudden, his feet collapsed through a dense pile of leaves, causing him to vanish as he fell down into a hidden pit in the top of the cliff. He grunted repeatedly as he quickly tumbled downwards, falling deeper and deeper into this strange abyss, until all lights went out.

A bright and vibrant forest spanned out in all directions, its trees tall and twisting, and littered with the multicolored leaves of an early autumn that gracefully swayed down and around. Beautiful looking birds danced and sang amongst the high branches. Most ordinary folk would feel a relaxing sense of serenity in such an environment, but no peace presently existed beneath the canopy.

A single, solitary eye stared up from the lowly ground. Faded, motionless, lifeless. Though as this eye's fixed gaze continued to try and prolong the canvas of its final sight into eternity, it was greeted by neither the bright blue skies, nor the twinkling heavens. Instead, someone else was looking back. A young girl named Ari stared down. And her blue eyes glistened more than the shiniest days of spring, while her long, soft hair rested darker than the blackest of nights. Her face was smooth and elegant, but her eyes... erratic, wide, dripping.

The rest of the head and body to whom the lonely eye belonged were now buried under a heaping pile of stones. The process for doing so had been quite painstaking, and had left Ari's hands filthy and blistered. Still though, it had also been incredibly simple; pick up a rock and let it go, rinse and repeat from head to toe, save for the small space over the eye that Ari had very intentionally left uncovered thus far.

She took many fast but deep breaths, her body trembling all over. She knew what she had done. In yet another fit of uncontrollable, feral craving and hunger, she had murdered a poor, innocent boy. A complete and utter stranger, with a life, a family, and most of all a story. A story that many out there in the world must surely know the beginning and middle of, but not the end.

"Only I will ever know that..." Ari felt herself nearly collapse as the reality of her actions battered through the walls of denial her mind had constructed in an effort to withstand the unending onslaught of guilt that was currently overwhelming her. Images of the trauma this boy and the few victims who came before him had experienced, as well as the inevitable suffering of those who cared about them flashed through her mind like the worst kinds of night terrors, only she knew she was awake.

"Why... why me... why can't I stop!" she whispered before screaming into the air. Grief, and hatred for her actions and herself washed over her like tidal waves over sand castles. "It's not my fault!" Ari said in a panic. Afterall, she had almost no memory of the murder. She just knew her mind was gone whenever it had happened. Like always, it had been wickedly laid to rest by an abhorrent and mysterious curse that forced her to commit such vile acts of evil. And as far as Ari knew, this curse was as much a part of her person as her very own blood and bones.

Nights where Ari woke up in a cold sweat with her heart pounding were practically a regular occurrence, but no amount of terrible dreams could ever train her to feel accustomed to the real act of taking a completely innocent person's life. And in a way, she was sort of thankful for that. Over the years, Ari had come to believe that evil was rooted deeply in the hearts of many. Child abductors, serial killers, genocidal dictators; the guilt she was feeling now was the one thing that separated her from those kinds of people. Or at least that's what she always told herself.

Ari continued to look down at the unburied eye. With each passing second, her memory of the boy's face seemed to fade, or perhaps repress away more and more. She took a selfish kind of comfort in that, for she couldn't bear to see him anymore. She only hoped that if there was even the tiniest remaining semblance of lifeforce left in the dry husk beside her feet, then maybe, just maybe, he could see her instead. And that if he saw how broken she was, he may yet forgive her. Her tears continued to streak down her face, faster and faster, one by one, until a few of them managed to drop off of her chin and land straight in the boy's eye. For a short moment, it looked as if he was crying too.

Ari let out a loud wail and shut her eyes tightly before dropping to her knees in a flash and forcing the last rock into place. The deed was done; she had sealed his fate twice. She slowly rose back to her feet, and winced when a wave of regret consumed her thoughts. She regretted volunteering to be the one to fetch supplies from the market that day. She regretted leading this sweet boy on when he offered to help pay for her things. She regretted believing that she was ever in control of her sick and evil curse.

A soft breeze gently brushed Ari's bangs back and forth, while a shaded sun casted its rays on her. What Ari regretted most of all though... was just how good she was feeling.

Ari had been feeling a powerful energy coursing through her blood ever since she'd regained conscious-ness. She felt strength in her bones, and all physical pain, even the throbbing guilt induced aches in her chest began to vanish. The fresh air around her tasted delectable, and the light of the sun seemed to wrap itself around her like a warm and thick blanket. In spite of the immense turmoil in her heart, Ari still felt all but reborn. It was the cruel twist of irony of her curse, and she was helpless to stop it. It made for such a surreal sensation, as if her euphoria was at war with her morality.

Ari knew how wholly undeserved her pleasure was; how stolen it had been. She dug her pointed fingernails into the bare flesh of her arm, clawing herself across its length while groaning heavily in an effort to make penance. The pain felt so numb, and hardly any blood was drawn.

The wind had already blown a bunch of leaves over the grave. She knew he might never be found, but even if he was, there would still be no answers or closure for his loved ones. In that instant, her thoughts started to disappear. Her whole mind seemed to fade away, and was replaced by nothing more than a potent desire to be alone and away from the world. Ari looked up from the ground, and into the vast yet empty expanse of forestry beyond. A familiar idea appeared in her head, and she could feel its temptation whispering into her ear like a demon on her shoulder, ushering her forward. She stepped past the grave, and walked off into the woods in the complete opposite direction of her home. Slowly, hopelessly, but with one destination in mind.

Ari walked in silence, her eyes flickering shut repeatedly, and for progressively longer intervals. Her sense of time completely dissipated; she didn't know for how long she had been walking or for how far, but eventually, she caught sight of what she was looking for. Beyond a cluster of low bushes ahead, sat the entrance to a small cave that emerged from the base of a cliff. Ari gazed into the mouth of the dark tunnel from afar, and could feel it calling to her. She had been to this cave many times before. It was a quiet, secluded little hideaway that none of her friends knew about, and she often ran to it whenever she wanted to disappear for some time. It was like her own private world, where neither punishment nor forgiveness existed.

Ari slowly waded through the thicket, and stepped through the entrance of the cave without so much as a glance over her shoulder. The light from outside, as well as the peaceful sounds of nature quickly disappeared behind her the further she walked into the cavern. It was almost pitch black now, and the only noise to be heard was the sound of her soft breathing. With a rueful chuckle, Ari closed her eyes tightly and spread her arms out wide before flopping down onto the ground. She landed with a hard crash on the rocks below, but didn't care about the pain.

Ari laid there on the rough, lumpy ground for what felt like an age. After a while, she thought it may be time to leave. She wondered how soon the sun would set; her friends would surely worry if she wasn't back before nightfall.

Her friends. Their faces suddenly flashed into Ari's mind, but something was wrong with them. Their appearances were blurry, distorted, and just barely recognizable. Ari concentrated, but her mental image didn't become any clearer. Instead, another figure appeared beside her friends. His face was equally blurred, but Ari still knew who she was looking at. He was the same boy she'd just finished burying. Ari winced, and watched as he and her friends all started to slowly fade out of her mind's eye; out of the cold and lonely world she now resided in.

"Never again..." Ari whispered into the abyss. As she continued to rest with her eyes closed, her other senses began to slip away, until she could perceive nothing aside from the pain in her heart. That pain gave way to a strange sense of belonging in this cave, as if she deserved to be in it. The rock under her back slowly began to feel more appropriate. She knew she didn't want to get up.

No one and nothing existed for Ari anymore. The rocky surface beneath her back, the chilly air of the cavern, the tingling of a spider crawling across her neck, she felt none of it. Her mind remained empty, with no thoughts of any nature drifting in or out. Even her own breath had become so hushed that not even an attentive bat would be able to hear it. For all intents and purposes, Ari was gone.

That is until... something hit her forehead. A small droplet that splattered on impact. At first, she didn't even notice it, but after a second, there was another, then another. The sensation eventually jolted Ari back to awareness. Her eyes begrudgingly fluttered open, and she sat up from her resting point on the ground to witness a startling sight. Right above her, seemingly trapped in the ceiling somehow, was someone else. Ari let out a gasp of fear and sprung to her feet. She tried to make out the person's features, but their face and body were partially obscured by layers of rock and dirt that cradled them in place.

"H-hello?" she called out nervously, but was met with no reply. With great caution, she advanced toward the person in the ceiling. She reached up to where their face was, and grazed her hand over their cheek. She could feel a wet substance creep onto her fingers, but still, the person gave no response of any kind.

Ari reached for their waist, and with a spurt of strength and courage, she heaved them out of the ceiling. A thin ray of daylight emerged from the hole they were stuck in, as dirt and rocks collapsed down onto the ground. Ari struggled to keep whoever this person was from toppling onto her. Once she found her balance, she gently lowered them down onto the rocks below, taking care to rest their head in her arm. She anxiously took her first clear look at who this was. The person was a brown-haired boy, likely around her age. His eyes were shut, and his face was cut and bruised all over, with streams of blood both dry and fresh trickling down his cheeks. His skin was pale enough to make him look like a corpse, and Ari shook as his bizarre and unexpected appearance made her wonder if she herself was now dead.

She started to examine the rest of the boy's body, before gasping again as she saw a gruesome stab wound in his side covered in dirt and clotted blood. Ari started to panic, and hastily tore off pieces of his shirt and bandaged the wound as well as she could. She pressed her hands against it hard, but she knew that without proper care he would never survive.

Ari lowered her ear down to his heart, but heard nothing. She took a deep breath to try and calm herself, and focused all her attention, all her hope on finding a heartbeat. After a short moment, she heard the faintest of thumping noises. He was somehow still alive, but just barely. Ari felt so helpless, so worthless, until a crazy idea clicked in her head. She could still feel the stolen strength and energy flowing throughout herself. With one arm wrapped behind his neck and head, and the other pressing tightly on his wound, she gently raised the boy's face up to hers, until their lips were mere inches apart.

"Please let me help... just this once," she said to herself. And with that, Ari pressed her lips against his own, focused as much of her power as she could muster, and began to blow softly into his mouth. A bright blue and orange glow from an otherworldly, mist-like substance sparked up around their mouths and throats. It traveled its way through their lips, from her body into his.

Ari kept this up for a while, until she felt almost all of the power within her falter, and she was forced to pull away. She started to cough violently, a weak and sickly feeling having rapidly overtaken her. But as she shook off the pain, and pressed her ear back against the boy's chest, she heard the thump of his heartbeat again, only this time it was much stronger. He was still unconscious, and covered in a myriad of cuts, bruises, and scrapes, but in that moment, she knew he would live.

Ari began to weep again, but unlike before, she now did so for neither grief nor punishment. Her body ached and pained all over, her strength almost completely depleted. But in her heart, she felt better.

Chapter Two
Glistening in the Dark

Ronin's eyes groggily blinked open and shut; back and forth and back again as the world slowly came into view. A flicker of light was the first thing he saw, but even its modest brightness was enough to keep his sensitive eyes squinting for a moment. He was lying on his back, with his head elevated and his arms down by his sides, and with some fluffy bedding beneath him. He attempted to sit up, but paused as he felt a sudden and intense pain in his side. He looked down at himself, and saw that his shirt was missing, and that several large bandages were wrapped around his waist.

"What's going on...?" he thought to himself.

He reached down to trace his fingers over the wound, and in that instance, memories began to pour into his mind. He recalled being chased into the woods, even being stabbed by that strange man, but everything after that was hazy. His head throbbed as he tried to fill in the blanks. Ronin had no idea where he was, who had helped him, or if he was even really being helped.

"Am I really awake?" he couldn't help but ask out loud. With another painful groan, he forced himself to sit up and raise his head. It took a lengthy moment for his blurry and double vision to straighten itself out, but it eventually gave view to the room around him.

As it turned out, Ronin was resting in a small bed in a corner of a room which looked a lot more like some bizarrely eccentric woodland lodge than any sort of medical facility. Dark plank wood made up most of the foundation, but the decor looked oddly fancy, with detailed art pieces lining the walls, and well-crafted cloths of various blacks, purples, and blues, covering most of the furniture. Compared to most of the old and rundown buildings he was used to spending time in, a place like this made him feel lost, confused, and utterly out of his element.

Anxiously, Ronin grit his teeth, and somehow managed to force himself out of bed. This made the pain in his side spike even harder, but given how deep his attacker's blade must have stabbed, Ronin was sincerely baffled that he could even stand at all.

"How long was I out for?" he wondered, figuring it must have been at least a few days.

The rest of the room was dark, with its distinct color choice not doing a very good job of helping to illuminate it from the thin and dim rays of light that creeped in through a few small shuddered windows. Ronin guessed the time must be early evening. He walked around the place, carefully examining the surface of it for clues as to who may be around. He opened up a large wardrobe on the wall beside his bed but regretted the decision fairly quickly, as right inside were rows of elegant looking dresses, as well as several other more intimate women's garments. He promptly shut the dresser with an embarrassed shake of his head.

"Am I in a... noblewoman's room?" he thought to himself. Such a possibility made Ronin worry that the bandages around his waist were not there out of charity. If whatever family who had helped him was expecting some kind of honorable tribute, they would surely be disappointed, and Ronin would be forced to repay his debt via servitude.

The next thing that caught Ronin's attention was a large table in the center of the room with a handful of books stacked on top of it. Their covers were all made from an old, scratched leather, and looked as if they were fighting a losing battle to hold the pages in place. He opened a book from the top of the stack. The pages were quite faded, and had mild tears littered throughout them. As he skimmed through, what he saw quickly caused his mild anxiety to evolve into chilling dread.

Page after page of text, written in strange characters from a language he didn't recognize in the slightest. What he could understand at least somewhat though, were the many pictures and diagrams that went alongside them. People were drawn in expressive, combative stances, and from their bodies emerged horrific powers. Lightning, fire, tendrils, smoke, blood, and more all shot forth in depictions of carnage and devastation. As he looked on, even more unsettling images showed up. Rituals, sacrifices, summonings, literal embodiments of unholy nightmares that somehow seemed to be plastered across the pages.

"Th-this can't be. The church swore it was all myth..." Ronin thought as his shaking hands dropped the book to the floor. The ruling church of Rendolyn vehemently denied the existence of legitimate witchcraft, but myth or not, such strong fascination with the fabled dark arts was considered highly disrespectful to their word, and would often be punished severely. Most ordinary people would never dare possess such texts. Ronin immediately lost all focus on his predicament, and instead let out a weak chuckle as he desperately tried to come up with a rational explanation for what he'd just seen. *"There are many languages I can't read. Surely this must be a fiction tale, or a historic text,"* Having completely forgotten the pain he was feeling, Ronin held a hand to his face and paced in circles around the table, his thoughts slowly turning into soft whispers.

"Maybe it's just some bizarre art?!" No matter how much he tried to deny it, the pictures in the book reminded him of the stories he'd heard from stubborn and old-fashioned elders when he was a little boy. Stories of evil, demonic things that thrived in the obscure crevices of the world that humanity was not welcome in. Ronin gently rubbed his cheek, reminding himself of the many times he'd been struck by a priest or nun when he dared to speak of such legends in their presence. They assured him that belief in these stories was madness, and as a frightened child, this was one of the few things they said that Ronin found himself wishing he could actually believe.

"Those lunatics wouldn't tell the truth even if they had their limbs tied to frightened horses," Ronin whispered to himself some more, but promptly shut up as he heard the crunching tread of shoes over leaves nearby. He looked at the windows again, and realized that someone was walking around outside the building, and from the sound of it, they were just about to pass the windows.

Ronin quickly crouched to hide behind the table cloth. The footsteps approached closer, and Ronin held his breath, waiting for whoever was there to pass by. A second later though, the footsteps stopped entirely, and a nerve-wracking silence persisted. Then, the footsteps returned, but were much louder and faster now before soon disappearing again, as if whoever was outside had suddenly sprinted away. Ronin stood back up, breathing heavily as he started to panic. Rational or not, any explanation he could currently come up with for what was going on seemed risky at best; he wanted to run.

The windows looked too small for him to squeeze through, which left a door across the room as his only escape route. Ronin dashed over to it as quietly as he could, but just as he was about to turn the handle, the door swiftly shot open in his direction. The solid wood slammed into his face, and sent him collapsing down with a painful bang of his head against the floor. Ronin went faint for a bit, but when he came to, it was from the sounds and feelings of him being dragged across the floor by his arms. He gasped loudly as his eyes shot open wide, and he felt a rush of energy spike through his veins. He yanked himself forward with all his might, and heard a similar gasp from someone else behind him. He rose to his feet again and shakily turned around.

Standing before him was a girl. She wore a long red cloak over one of the dark dresses he had seen earlier, and looked at him with a mix of caution and surprise. Ronin tried to avoid panicking any further, but he knew that his worry was plastered all over his face. She couldn't possibly be a real... one of them. Neither of them spoke a word right away, but eventually the girl slowly started to take a small step forward.

"Stay away!" shouted Ronin as he gave in to his fear and moved back behind the table to put something between them. He looked around for any sort of weapon to defend himself with, but saw nothing and opted to instead raise his fists as menacingly as a skinny, very clearly wounded person could hope for.

The girl shook surprisedly at Ronin's aggression. She kept her focus on him, and continued to move slowly until her foot collided with the book Ronin had dropped on the floor earlier. He watched her sneak a quick glance at it, then look back to him, her face now full of embarrassment.

"Oh my! I am terribly sorry this is all a grave misunderstanding! I promise I mean you no harm!" she exclaimed while shooting her hands beside her face in a sign of peace.

"You-you're a witch!?" Ronin half asked and half exclaimed. He was unable to hide the terror in his voice as he dared to utter the word. The girl's jaw dropped at his accusation, and her expression turned frightful. She said nothing for a while, seemingly unsure of how to respond.

"W-what?! Are you mad?!" she asked with clear shock in her voice. "Of course I'm no witch!"

"Then why do you have these books?!" Ronin demanded to know as he picked another one up off the table and held it open to her. "If the church found out about them, you'd be locked away and receive more lashes than they have pages!"

"They're not what you think. They're just... art history books..." the girl answered meekly. Ronin scowled at her, before throwing the book at her face as hard as he could. The girl yelped, and when she moved her hands in front of her face to block it, Ronin quickly turned to run back towards the open door. He was only a few feet away from escape, when for the shortest second, Ronin thought he saw a bizarre, dark mist or cloud shaped thing fire past him before vanishing. He didn't have time to think about it though, as all of a sudden, the door slammed shut with such force that it was nearly blown off its hinges.

Ronin stumbled back in surprise before falling to the floor again. He spun himself around and backed up as far as he could until he felt his bare back press against the cold wall. He looked up to see the girl aiming her open hand in his direction. She looked nearly as distressed as he was too.

"What was that?!" Ronin shouted as he closed his eyes and hid behind his arms like a child.

"I'm sorry!" said the girl.

"Please... just let me go," Ronin begged.

"I just need you to listen to me for a moment," she replied while moving slightly closer. "I know that 'witch' isn't exactly the most flattering term to go by these days. If you'd prefer you could call me a mage or sorceress, or something like that!"

"I don't care what you're called! Just don't make my skin melt off or anything!"

"Look! You can trust me I swear. Those books are wholly outdated, like hundreds of years outdated," the girl pleaded desperately. "They're more akin to history textbooks than guides these days to be honest. You won't find any hex dolls or disgusting cauldrons in this home," she continued with a forced laugh, but Ronin still refused to believe her.

"I understand why you're afraid, but to be fair, I did save your life already. It took me almost an entire day until sunset to drag you here from that cave!" she said while gesturing to his bandages. Ronin looked at his wound again, and was finally reminded of the horrible pain it was causing him that had only been accentuated by his aggressive movements. He gripped his side tight, then looked back at the girl who was trying so desperately to ease his nerves. She had a pretty, decorative flower clipped to her hair above the smooth skin of her face, and her figure was slim and elegant. In fact, she looked quite beautiful, far more so than he ever would've expected from a witch.

The last of his strength evaporated, and Ronin shuddered in place as the girl carefully moved over to him with her hands raised up again. He looked away as she stood above him, unsure of what to expect, when out of the corner of his eye, he saw her reach down and offer him a hand. He slowly turned to look up at her. Her crystal blue eyes were wide and bright, and her lips remained still, uttering no curses.

"My name's Ariana, or Ari for short," she said with a pleasant smile.

"Ronin... " he mumbled. He did not accept her hand.

"I'm sorry?"

"Ronin, it's my name," he clearly answered.

"It's lovely to meet you Ronin," she replied with a light hearted giggle that added to his confusion.

"Are you going to hurt me?" he asked anxiously.

"Not unless you try to hurt me..." she answered. Ronin struggled to imagine how she could possibly feel threatened by someone in his position, but the answer soon hit him.

"The church would probably silence me before they'd even find you if I ran into town screaming witch so... that sounds like a good deal to me," he conceded. Ari nodded, seemingly giving him as much approval as she could afford to. Ronin shared a little of her sentiment even if he was still far from trusting her. He'd been begging for his life this entire time, and in all fairness, he still had it, he reckoned. "What happens now then?" Ronin asked.

"Well for starters I thought I'd help you up, but you don't seem entirely on board with that plan," answered Ari as she took a seat on the floor ahead of him.

"I haven't forgotten the stories... of what your kind do to people, and those books-"

"Are again wholly outdated!" Ari interrupted. "I'm honestly shocked you're even able to fathom a witch's existence. Haven't you learned not to trust everything you hear in stories? For goodness' sake that's why the world at large hardly even believes we exist these days," said Ari resentfully. "Contrary to what those over-zealous, fanatical priests and inquisitors may have you believe, witches are real. But we certainly aren't all about evil curses and demonic worship anymore... or well at least most of us aren't."

Ronin opened his lips to respond to her, but only more painful grunts escaped his mouth.

"Look, you're very injured and obviously can't just stay there on the floor. If I try to help you back into bed, are you going to throw something at me again?" asked Ari with her arms crossed. Ronin shook his head. Ari moved to wrap his arm over her shoulder to help him walk back across the room to the bed he had awoken in. Once he got settled, she went to pull up a chair.

"So, I take it you probably have a lot of questions?" she asked.

"I don't even know where to begin," replied Ronin. He was feeling a little bit calmer now.

"Understandable... well, long story short, yesterday I found you all but dead from that stab wound in a cave, and I managed to patch you up and drag you back here, where you've been passed out ever since. Welcome to my humble coven!" Ari cheered.

"Yesterday? You mean I was unconscious for just one night?"

"Yes, oddly enough. If I hadn't been so sure you'd be passed out for at least a few days, I would have cleaned my room right away. I guess you're tougher than you look." Ari playfully flicked his arm.

"I certainly don't feel very tough right now. You said this place is a coven. Are there more of you?"

"Yes. There's me and two other witches here. And now that you're awake, please try to stay behaved and avoid screaming anymore... the others weren't very keen on the idea of my bringing home a guest."

Ronin paused for a moment, taking time to steady his breathing and rest his aching body against the soft cushions. Their fluffiness felt almost surreal, in his mind at least. In less than an hour, Ronin felt that he had made more memories than the last entire year of his life, for better or for worse. Whereas each monotonous day on the road felt like the same few identical seconds stretched out over endless hours, with little more to occupy his mind other than figuring out what to eat and where to sleep, this day so far made him feel like an entirely different person. For a short moment, he struggled to recall just what exactly he was doing with himself before today, when his hand started to reach down to where his bag would ordinarily be.

"Where are my belongings?" he asked, his voice back to being worried as he realized he didn't have his handcloth with him. Ari frowned.

"Oh... well you had a few coins in your pocket when I found you but other than that I saw nothing. I'm sorry. Were they important?" Ronin took another long pause and shifted his gaze away from her. He must have lost his bag at some point during the fight or his fall into the cave. A part of him wanted to go and look for it straight away, but he worried that like always, luck would not be on his side. He felt his heart shatter as he realized that all of his efforts and hardships in searching for his long-lost family had probably been for nothing.

"Not anymore..." he muttered before letting loose a heavy sigh. A stretch of silence followed.

"Well... " began Ari. "May I ask you something then?" Ronin gave her a slight nod. "What happened to you?"

"I'm uh, not entirely sure to be honest. Someone tried to mug or kidnap me, I guess? The man was pretty persistent; he chased me out of town."

"Sounds like you need to be more careful," teased Ari.

"Easy for you to say. Not all of us can conjure balls of fire, or turn our enemies into frogs. And I still defeated him by the way."

"Good grief, just what exactly do you think magic even is?" asked Ari with an eyeroll as Ronin referenced even more misconceptions of witches.

"Um, well... I guess I have no clue."

"Well, you weren't entirely wrong. Simply put, magic exists in various schools, and those with an affinity for the arcane arts can manipulate the energies of whichever school they are born into, to cast spells. There's pyromancy, illusory, necromancy, you get the idea," said Ari as if what she was describing was as simple to understand as different kinds of fruit.

"I'm not sure what to think about any of that... what school are you from?" asked Ronin. Ari chuckled and gave him a sly smirk. She stood up beside his bed, one hand rested on the post, the other raised up before his eyes. She snapped her fingers. All of a sudden, the room went pitch black. Ronin nearly jumped out of his skin. The room had become unnaturally dark, as if they were trapped in a bottomless abyss in which no light could reach. His anxiety shot right back up, as he frantically looked around the place until something caught his attention. The windows were still in view, and he could see the sunlight shining from outside the shudders, but still, he couldn't see anything in the room itself. It was as if every object around them had lost its ability to reflect light.

"Illathum noctalis," said an invisible Ari proudly. "Shadow magic."

Her voice startled Ronin, but he calmed down as he realized she meant him no harm. A strange, unfamiliar sensation started to dawn on him. As he sat there in pure darkness, he could feel his pain slightly be eased. His body felt lighter somehow, and his energy was partially renewed, but most bizarrely of all, was a mysterious tingling he felt in his eyes. Despite there still not being even the faintest shimmer of light in the room, his vision gradually adjusted. Himself, the bed, the walls and decor, it all faded back into sight, until he looked up, and was met by the gaze of Ari, still smirking at him.

She let out a loud gasp as they made eye contact. Her face looked more surprised than even Ronin had been a moment ago. She jumped back away from him in shock, knocking over her chair as she did so.

"W-what is happening?!" she asked.

"What do you mean?! Didn't you do this?" asked Ronin as her reaction made him start to panic again.

"No! I mean, yes I darkened the room but... your eyes," she stuttered. Ronin's eyes were clear and glistening; enough for Ari to see her own reflection in them, and he could see the same in hers.

"You can see me!"

If there was one thing Ronin learned about Ari during the short evening in which they'd met, it was just how stubborn she could be. For reasons concerning both of their safety, she was understandably reluctant to let him leave right away, though she fortunately wasn't the type to cuff him to the bed either. After a quarrelsome back and forth discussion, she persuaded him to spend the night. Ronin felt a little bad about taking Ari's bed, but she insisted, and the rest was soothing and desperately needed even regardless of his injuries. He didn't want to admit to Ari or even really himself that the warm blanket and soft pillows he had been nearly snuggling in during their talk had done a far better job of persuading him to stay than anything she'd said to convince him. He slept for many hours, and even remained beneath the covers for one more after awakening. It had taken him years to become accustomed to sleeping with a lumpy bag and withered cloak, and just one single night in this coven to ruin all that hard work.

Presently, a bright sun shined in through the now fully open windows, showing the room in a new light from what Ronin had seen it in yesterday. It actually managed to look a lot homier than before. He sat up and noticed a small table that had been moved to his bedside. Placed on top of it were a tall glass of water, some sliced bread and cheese, and a tiny note.

"Meet me outdoors when you're ready. I left you some fresh clothes by the door!" It was signed by Ari.

"Wait... was I practically naked that whole time?!" Ronin said aloud. He figured there was no way he couldn't have noticed something like that, but embarrassment washed over his face when a quick lift of the blankets confirmed his fears.

After aggressively wolfing down his breakfast, Ronin rose from bed to find that the pain in his side was mostly gone. He pressed his hand against the bandaged wound, and felt nothing more than a slight pinch. He then carefully unwrapped the bandages. Aside from a nasty scar and some dried-up blood, there was little to worry about.

"What did that witch...er... girl do to me?" Ronin was baffled as yet another addition was made to the headache inducing swarm of questions he still had.

He found his clothes hung up on the door handle. They consisted of a new black travel cloak, alongside a white tunic with beige trousers. To some people, these clothes might not look very different from any ordinary attire, but as Ronin traced his fingers over the fabric of the tunic, he felt a distinctly familiar smoothness to it.

"Silk?! How rich are these people?!" All of a sudden Ronin felt very reluctant to take the clothes, but did so anyway seeing as how he had nothing else to wear. He carefully dressed himself, hoping that whoever this attire belonged to wouldn't be expecting it returned, then turned to leave the room.

He soon found himself in a narrow hallway, and followed it until he arrived at a larger space that he guessed was a common room of sorts. Bookshelves lined the thick and tall walls, and in the center was a smoothed-out tree stub that served as a table. The room also contained a roaring fireplace, as well as a fancy chandelier that in his mind would be far better suited for a queen's ballroom than a crammed and secluded witch's lair.

"Mercy on my soul. I must be dreaming," came a sudden and aggravated voice. Ronin spun around in place to see a new girl sitting in a large armchair across the room from him. She had golden hair beneath a tall hat, and wore a dark purple and white dress that was similar to Ari's, but she came off as far less inviting.

"Oh um, pardon me miss. I've honestly been wondering the same thing myself," excused Ronin anxiously.

"Be silent, or you'll soon wish that were the case," she said strictly. "You must be that helpless sap whom Ariana brought here the other day. Her disdain for our rules is no surprise, but frankly I at least expected her to maintain a higher standard for her tastes." Ronin stood in place, stuttering incoherently under his breath as he felt any sense of comfort around witches Ari had given him evaporate in an instant

"Oh, leave the poor boy alone, Elena," came a different voice as a boy walked into the room through another doorway. In contrast to the others Ronin had met so far, this platinum blonde haired boy donned a brown robe. He turned to Ronin and briefly sized him up before chuckling. "Look at him, I never imagined there was someone out there even scrawnier than I am. He'd make for an awfully boring foe but a still half-decent butler I'd reckon. What threat could he possibly pose?"

"He has borne witness to our livelihoods and home. That alone is dangerous enough. I would think you of all people would be aware of that, Jeremiah." The boy's jovialness briefly flickered away at her words, and he scowled at the girl he called Elena before composing himself.

"Oh, wow say my full name, I'm oh so intimated," he replied sarcastically as he stepped over to Ronin. "Don't worry mate, if she decides to kill you so haphazardly, I'll make sure to pour extra salt in her tea tonight." He gave Ronin a pat on the back that made the stressed-out boy jolt in place a bit. Jeremiah then walked away, leaving Elena behind to groan in annoyance.

"Listen here whatever your name is, I am Archwitch Elena, and this is my home you stand in," she declared. Elena then rose from her seat and walked over to Ronin. She flicked her wrist in front of him so that her open palm was just beneath his chin. Ronin's eyes went wide, and he felt his heartbeat triple in the span of a second as he watched a small, crackling orb of lightning manifest on top of her palm. The thought of it touching him made Ronin almost wish that being stabbed had finished him for good.

"Look I didn't mean to intrude I just-"
"Shut. Up." Elena interrupted again. Ronin noticed that the lightning orb seemed to flare up bit by bit the angrier she got. He tried to calm his tense breathing and maintain a stoic appearance like he had trained himself to

do in dangerous situations, but inside his head he was silently pleading for Elena to back off. He felt like his years of experience in these kinds of intense confrontations had been scrubbed clean off his mind. In practice, a literal ball of lightning being held mere inches from his skin was completely incomparable to any blade.

"I want it to be perfectly clear that the only reason I am permitting you to stay here, or even survive for that matter, is due to the incessant begging of Ariana, a trusted if not rather naive friend of mine. She insists that there is something special about you, and that because of this, you will keep our secrets safe." Elena sighed visibly at her own words. Ronin suspected that her faith in Ari's promises was about as flimsy as his faith that Elena wouldn't suddenly change her mind at any moment and strike him down anyways.

"So, here's what happens now. You're going to walk outside, and Ariana is going to give you a test to prove her claim that you can in fact, perceive magic in the same way that the rest of us can. Afterwards, we can figure out what to do with you. Understood?" Elena asked. Ronin didn't answer her right away though, as his brain was far too busy working overtime to try and figure out if her question was rhetorical or not. Elena groaned some more, and finally waved her hand down and vanished away the lightning orb. Once she finished, Ronin released what was quite possibly the largest exhale of relief in his entire life, much to Elena's disgust.

"I'm sorry! I'm sorry, okay?! I promise I don't want to cause any trouble; I mean what could I do to all of you that wouldn't end up causing something far worse to happen to me, right? Also, I'm really thankful for my life being saved, I never truly believed witches were evil, and I have a lot of street skills so I'm sure I can pay you back somehow-" Ronin continued to helplessly babble out increasingly incoherent promises and questions, both in an effort to relieve some of the tension he was still feeling, and to futilely try and make Elena less inclined to sear his flesh. He was finally silenced when Elena forced one hand over his mouth, and facepalmed with her other.

"Just... go," she said through gritted teeth before turning around and leaving him.

"Um, just one more question please? Sorry... " Ronin asked as he looked around and saw nothing but more hallways. Elena stopped in her tracks, but neither spoke nor turned to face him again. "Uh... how do I get outside?" he asked like a frightened child.

A loud slamming sound was heard as a powerful surge of wind blasted Ronin through the front door of the coven. He yelped in surprise and pain, and felt like a rag doll being tossed aside by a tornado as he tumbled down a small set of stairs before landing in a small stone courtyard. For a while, Ronin held still on the ground until he was certain that his impromptu introduction to Elena's air magic was over, but even then, he didn't get up right away. He instead opted to press his face against the cold floor of the courtyard, and just groan agitatedly in place for a bit.

"*The rats would never treat me like this...* " he thought.

Eventually, Ronin started to push himself up. When he raised his head, he was immediately startled by the gaze of Ari who was leaning over him. He quickly stumbled to his feet, nearly bumping his head into her in the process.

"You couldn't have helped me deal with your boss?!"

"Sorry! She insisted on having a more private talk with you first," answered Ari with embarrassment as she started to pat down his disheveled clothes and hair. "Would you believe me if I said she only did this because she cares?"

"Not really, no," replied Ronin as he shooed her hands away. "Anyways, what are we doing out here? Elena said you were going to test me or something."

"Straight to the point, eh? Very well, brace yourself!" Ronin watched confusedly as Ari proceeded to rest her arms firmly by her sides, and shut her eyes.

After a few deep breaths, Ari flicked her arms up high. As she did so, a swirling haze of black mist shot forth from the ground beneath their feet, twisting and wrapping over itself to create an ominous cloud around them that blocked out the sunlight. Ronin shook at first, but as he was buried alive by the shadows, he realized could still see every minute detail of the scenery inside it from the crinkled leaves to the old stone walkway. It all looked perhaps even slightly clearer than before.

"You have a gift," said Ari with excitement.

"No, I do not," replied Ronin defensively. "I can't possibly be a witch or whatever, I'm hardly even just a guy. This has to be your doing. I mean I have never in my life experienced anything like this before."

Ari lowered the cloud of darkness and gazed at him with a look of contemplation.

"I suppose it is quite strange... without a teacher it's unlikely that you ever would have learned how to use your abilities, but you still should've felt some passive, abnormal effects over the years. Vision in the dark, increased energy at night, sensitivity to light perhaps?"

"Nope, nothing like that at all," answered Ronin confidently. He could hardly rationalize the mere idea that he somehow possessed magical abilities. It was like being told he had an extra pair of arms attached to his body that he had simply never noticed before.

"Hmm... " mumbled Ari while holding her chin. "Aha! I've got it," she exclaimed before running off inside. A moment later she returned, and alongside her was the boy from earlier, Jeremiah.

"Alright Jey, just stand right here," she said while ushering the clearly irritated boy down to the bottom of the steps. She then leapt over to Ronin and stood beside him.

"Are you sure about this Ari?" Jey asked while raising his hands into an aggressive stance. "I mean I'm plenty happy to take a free shot at you of all people, but it doesn't sound particularly fair to him." He nodded towards Ronin.

"Positive Jey. Don't hold back!"

"Okay... but if Elena asks, just tell her you both drank foul water or something, got it?"

"Uh Ari, what exactly is going on here?" whispered Ronin as he elbowed her.

"Just a little experiment, don't worry," she answered before promptly shutting her eyes. From Jey's readied hands, a blinding orb of light emerged that rapidly grew in size and intensity. Ronin instinctively shut his eyes the moment he saw it. Still though, he felt stranger sensations begin to overtake him. His body began to ache and sting all over, and he soon found it difficult to breathe. He could feel the light's power coil its way around him like a snake gradually squeezing out his life. He collapsed down to his knees, prompting Jey to disperse the light orb. The bizarre sensations dissipated as quickly as they appeared, much to Ronin's relief. Despite the process being painful, he hadn't feared for his life the same way he had when talking to Elena, though that didn't make this experience any less aggravating.

After taking a moment to pull himself together, Ronin stood back up with half a mind to snap at Ari, but he hesitated when he saw that she too was pulling herself up from the ground, and looked to be equally strained.

"There... b-believe me now?" she asked through deep pants. Ronin looked at her in disbelief.

"She's telling the truth mate," said Jey with a giddy smile spread over his face. "That was no ordinary light, it was a luminosity orb that can only be summoned by someone able to wield light magic, like me. And it can only do that kind of damage to those of the shadow school. Like you two."

Ari and Ronin stood back up and dusted off some leaves and dirt.

"I still don't get it though... " began Ronin. "Why am I just now feeling these powers?"

"I can't say," replied Ari. "But regardless, these abilities of yours are incredible, but dangerous. You need a teacher." Ronin stared at her wordlessly as he struggled to decide how he felt about all of this. Everything Ari was saying to him made Ronin feel so detached from who he thought he was, as if his mind had somehow fled from his body and taken over the identity of someone else.

"You realize that if you ask Elena to let him study here, she'll probably fry your flesh to a crisp, then blast you all the way to the capital, right?" interjected Jey. His words sounded mostly hyperbolic to Ronin, but at the same time quite believable.

"Perhaps, but you have my back right, Jey? You can persuade her to be gentle like always," said Ari while giving him a sly wink. Jey only sighed in response, holding his face in one hand.

"Fine, I'll help you. But the next time you come to me for a favor, you better be carrying a heaping bag of Sorem's potions to compensate me for the horrendous ordeal I'm about to endure," snarked Jey as he walked back inside.

Ronin saw a lonely stone bench across the courtyard, and walked over to it to take a much-needed seat. He leaned his head back to look up at the open sky through the tree line, and paced his breaths to try and soothe the throbbing in his head from all the information he was trying to process.

"So, what will you do?" Ari asked as she sat beside him.

"I don't know," Ronin answered.

"I know this is a lot to take in, but magic is such a rare and powerful birthright." Ronin said nothing in response. He simply continued to stare off into the distorted clouds above. "It's not as if your whole life would have to be upended. You could take some books home with you and visit for lessons." Ronin could tell that was a blatant and desperate lie. His brief exchange with Archwitch Elena made that clear enough. He finally turned to look at her.

"Why do you care so much?" Ronin asked. His question clearly caught Ari off guard, and she stumbled while looking away from him.

"I um... I've never met anyone else born with shadow magic... " she mumbled after a long pause. "And I was starting to think I never would." Ronin looked at her rather skeptically.

He then found his thoughts drawn back to the days prior to their meeting. He remembered what it had been like to aimlessly travel for months on end, searching anywhere and everywhere for clues that seemed non-existent. The world disappeared briefly for Ronin, and all he could see was his family crest, its proud raven slowly withering away into shriveled remains. He instinctively reached a hand behind himself to where his pack would have been, and felt his heart wince as his grasp touched nothing other than his shirt. His mental image of the crest continued to fade away, and by some force in his mind unbeknownst to him, he willed it to go faster.

"I'll stay here," he said abruptly. Ronin didn't look at Ari, but somehow, he knew that she was smiling quite happily.

Chapter Three
Am I Welcome in Your World?

"Please, do try to remain calm. The easiest way to mess up is to lose all of your momentum," said Ari cheerfully.

"How could I possibly lose something I never had to begin with?" Ronin replied with irritation. "It feels like you've had me doing nothing but studying and meditating this whole time. I'm no more prepared for learning magic than some back alley-cockroach." Ari smirked.

"Oh my, I am truly scared to wonder what must have happened to you if you ever spoke to your school teachers with such a tone."

Twice had the sun rose and set since Ronin began lurking amidst his newfound companions, following the teachings of Ari in the ways of shadow magic. As Ari and Jeremiah had predicted, Archwitch Elena was anything but pleased when they proposed their plan to her, but reluctantly agreed to let Ronin stay and be trained under the condition that he would completely master all of the most barebones basics of magic before even considering any fully fledged spells. Thus, the fruit of Ronin's hard work had presently built up to the climactic step of 'putting out,' a light.

He and Ari sat across a table from each other inside a small study room. The blinds were drawn tight so as to block out the morning sun, leaving them in near complete darkness, save for the bright orange hue of a small candle perched atop a plate on the table. From it emitted just enough light to dimly illuminate their faces to the ordinary eye.

"You're overthinking it," said Ari, who seemed unable to fully understand just how obscure this task was for Ronin. "All you have to do is remove the light from the candle, but without extinguishing it. It's quite easy. Just feel your energy move from your mind, down through your arm, and into your fingertips as you twist the shadows around the light." As she spoke, Ari moved her hand in a fluent motion, wrapping the shadow cast from the candle itself into an eerie black sphere around the light until the two of them were brought to darkness. Ronin couldn't suppress the goosebumps he got whenever he watched Ari's masterful displays of her abilities. The shadows always seemed to take on an unnatural appearance whenever she toyed with them. Their otherwise semi-transparent and depthless shade was replaced by a darkness so thick that trying to see anything through it was as pointless as trying to look around with one's eyes closed, at least for any ordinary person.

"You say that as if you're teaching me to tie my shoes," groaned Ronin. Ari released her grip on the candle's shadow and motioned for him to try again. He took a deep breath, concentrated as hard as he could, and tried his best to copy her hand movements. The candle's shadow did nothing more than twitch ever so slightly, mimicking the motion of the flickering flame, and perhaps mocking Ronin in the process.

"Ah... may I see you do it again?" he asked regretfully.

"Very well, but you won't progress much if I give you the answers every time. Magic is quite intuitive, you sort of need to develop your own flow for it, you know?" Ronin said nothing back. "Besides, it's also somewhat taxing for me to demonstrate everything time and again. Magic is fueled by our own energy, which is expended when we cast spells."

"You're just moving a tiny shadow with your fingers. How draining could that possibly be?" asked Ronin doubtfully.

"Not much individually... but this is the twenty first time you've had me demonstrate," she answered with a slight chuckle.

"Not like anyone asked you to keep count... "

Ronin continued to tally up more and more failed attempts, being mostly unable to think of any ways to vary his approach to this challenge. Despite everything he had seen and felt in the past few days, the mere concept of magic still seemed entirely alien to him. He still felt as if he were being asked to do something that defied logic and possibility alike, even though Ari's repeated demonstrations proved otherwise.

"Ack!" he explained at the fortieth or so failed attempt. "This is hopeless. All I'm doing is waving my hands around like an idiot. There has to be some other trick to it!"

"I wish it were that simple, but the fact is that you've only just recently started trying to harness your power.

You just need to feel your energy click somehow, but unfortunately that may take some time. Have faith." Ironically, Ronin sort of figured that when faced with a seemingly impossible task, blind faith in success was possibly the strongest kind of motivation he could ever hope for. But Ronin was still struggling to believe in something as simple as the fact that he was currently staying in a house with two floors and multiple bedrooms, which left little room for faith in his possession of all powerful magic.

"Well, how long did it take for you to first accomplish any kind of spell cast?"

"Um... that's difficult to say for certain. I was very young," answered Ari bashfully.

"Great... " Ronin held his face. "May we take a break? I can't think straight anymore."

"Very well, but repetition is key. We'll try more later today."

The two of them then rose from their seats and drew back the blinds. Such a seemingly ordinary task now struck Ronin as being far more technical, and even philosophical than he ever could have imagined. He had learned from Ari that shadows and darkness acted as a kind of fuel source for shadow magic. They could either be manipulated directly, or have their combined power harnessed in order to cast greater, more mystical spells.

Shadows themselves however, of course cannot exist in the complete absence of light, which is where Ari taught him that shadows created beneath the light of the moon were the most powerful. This stood to reason that shadows cast from broad daylight were the weakest, but almost paradoxically, when he drew back the curtains, said daylight created dozens of more shadows throughout the room than there had previously been with just the candle. Ronin paused momentarily, concentrating as hard as he could to assess the quantity over quality and try to perceive any changes in his presumed power. But he felt nothing, something he was becoming all too familiar with lately, much to his frustration.

He and Ari headed back into the living room, from which Ari turned to depart down the hallway towards her bedroom.

"I've a few chores to attend to for now. What will you do?" she asked curiously, to which Ronin simply shrugged. Ari sighed ever so slightly. "I believe Elena is free at the moment, perhaps you could ask her to teach you some history?" she suggested quite optimistically.

"Pass. I've no desire for another flying lesson," said Ronin.

"Understandable, but it would still do you some good to spend more time outside of your quarters. You've been here for days now but I can't seem to recall seeing you talk with anyone besides me. There would be far less tension if the three of you got to know each other better."

"Ah... I'll get around to it." Ronin put in no effort to hide how reluctant he was feeling to do such.

"At least say hi to Jey. He has asked me to remind him of your name twice already," said Ari before leaving. Ronin let her go without another word. He didn't have the heart to tell Ari that he had also forgotten Jey's name up until now.

Once Ari was gone, Ronin immediately wanted to return to his room, as she had predicted. However, Ari's words of encouragement had gotten through to him at least a little bit, so he instead decided to linger around in the living room for a moment longer. Despite wanting to take a break from practicing magic, Ronin was still having a hard time finding other ways to occupy his mind. He had learned quickly that there was little happening around the coven that didn't end up tying back into the subject in one way or another. For example, the kitchen featured a perfectly functional brick oven, but the three witches that he now stayed with rarely ever bothered with flint and steel or other conventional means of actually lighting it. Instead, Elena would just toss a spark onto the fuel and conjure a roaring fire almost instantly.

Ronin's inability to distract himself from anything magic related was also his own fault though, even if it was because he was simply too fascinated by all of it. Though he had never been much of an academic, Ronin was unable to resist as his mind was allured to the myriad of implications brought by the mere existence of magic. While most witches were presumably quite secretive with their abilities and rarely used them to affect society, the world fundamentally could not function the way ordinary folk perceived it to if some select people were able to go around wielding bolts of lightning and balls of fire as easily as they could a knife and fork.

He recalled many of the famed and hyperbolic religious and folklore stories he had heard as a kid, and now wondered how many of them were more so misinterpreted than flat out made up. Ronin chuckled to himself as he realized that learning of the existence of such blasphemous magic ironically made him marginally more open minded to the presumed authenticity of the holy text far more than any nun or priest ever had.

He paced around the living room, taking glances at the many large and mildly dusty bookshelves that lined the tall walls. Even though most of the books themselves were written in archaic languages he didn't recognize, and the ones that weren't were filled with spell related vocabulary he was not yet familiar with, Ronin had still spent much of his free time over the past couple of days reading what he could by his lonesome. He kept searching through the plethora of volumes until one of the larger books caught his attention. He pried it from its tight spot in the shelf and dusted off the cover. *"Alerian Alexander's Anthologies of the Arcane: Volume III,"* read the title.

Ronin flipped through the pages and found that the book was a collection of various tales from the past couple of centuries. The pages were long and dense, and some of the stories told accounts of witches subtly influencing the lives of ordinary people via spells disguised as medicine or bizarre acts of nature. It was a wholesome if not probably biased and fabricated read. Despite what Ari had told him the day that they'd first met, about witches no longer existing to be wicked, he was still not so naive as to believe that magic was never used for greedy or nefarious purposes.

"I wouldn't have guessed you to be one fascinated by the old tales," came a firm but quiet voice from behind. Ronin glanced back over his shoulder and silently cursed Ari as he saw that Archwitch Elena was watching him from the head of the stairs. Her face was plain, and not necessarily accusatory, but her green eyes possessed an unwavering, near blink-less stare that reminded Ronin of the way town guards would sometimes glare at him.

"Why assume that? You don't know me."

Elena smirked slightly.

"Aye, and as strange as this may sound, that is precisely why I must make so many bold assumptions of you," she said. Ronin was unable to get a word in after as, much to his surprise, Elena suddenly vaulted over the railing in front of her and began to drop the ten or so feet down to the floor. With a swift hand motion, a strong gust of wind, carefully placed so as to avoid causing clutter in the room, cushioned her fall perfectly.

"Tell me, how goes your training?" she asked as she approached Ronin. Her question seemed innocent enough at surface level, but even Ronin could easily tell that she was more than just curious.

"Poorly, and that is still a generous term. You've nothing to worry about ma'am-"

"Elena, please," interrupted the Archwitch, who looked a little embarrassed at being addressed as ma'am by someone who was about the same age as her. She then turned away from Ronin and searched along the bookshelves until she located a few select volumes before handing them to him. "It's no surprise that someone of your age is having difficulty learning such eccentric concepts. Usually, we witches start our training as soon as we're barely old enough to walk and talk. Though I do suspect that in this case the fault may lie with your teacher just as much as yourself."

Ronin took the new books from her and flipped through the pages to find that they contained purely beginners' exercises. The techniques were so basic that they did not even pertain to any magic school in particular, and seemed far more attainable at a glance than the shadow school texts Ari had given him.

"Ariana was a child prodigy of her abilities, she doesn't know what it's like to struggle with magic. Her difficulties come from... different sources... " said Elena as she trailed off into thought momentarily. Ronin watched her in confusion for a few blank seconds before speaking up.

73

"I don't mean to be rude, but why are you helping me?" he asked. Elena shook her head as his question brought her back to attention.

"I simply believe that if you absolutely must stay here then your training should at least be handled properly," she answered defensively. Elena raised a hand to hold her face, as if her head ached painfully. Worried that she may be about to lash out at him again, Ronin closed the books she had given him and turned to leave, but made it no more than a few steps.

"Surely you must understand my trepidation at your presence? Do you not?" she asked him frustratedly. Ronin turned back to her with a puzzled expression on his face. The way she was asking him made it seem like she wanted his validation, strangely enough.

"I suppose I can relate to being wary of a stranger. Though perhaps not blasting them through a door," he answered.

"That was merely to get my point across, and you emerged unscathed." Elena crossed her arms. "That history book... " she continued. "It was first written nearly two hundred years ago, and the series has seven volumes in total. As far as I am aware, they make up nearly all of the surviving records of the actions of our kind for the time period, not just in this coven, but across all of our lairs hidden throughout the world. Have you any idea as to why this is the case?" Ronin shrugged.

"It is because our people had little time for book-keeping when we were being driven to near extinction in these lands. When the church rose to power by winning the minds of the masses, we were hunted down relentlessly for our 'devilish acts.' Only by hiding away from 'normal,' folk such as yourself can my friends and I hope to remain safe from such a fate." Elena took a deep breath and closed her eyes once she finished speaking. The subject was clearly not one she enjoyed approaching. Ronin on the other hand, felt offended by her words, and did what he could to restrain himself from scoffing at her.

"Please, don't affiliate me with the church, Rendolyn, or whatever other entities come to mind. I have been hunted for far less than devilry, and hold no loyalty to any powers in this world or the next." His words seemed to surprise Elena, who looked at him with an expression mixed between satisfaction and skepticism.

"Fair enough... though I certainly can't fully believe such a claim yet," she said, making Ronin sigh.

"There's nothing for me out there in the world, but here in this coven, I get a place to stay, meals to eat, and an admittedly rather interesting purpose for my life all of a sudden. I have no reason to give any of that up, or to endanger you." For a brief moment, Ronin thought he perceived the faintest hint of understanding in Elena's eyes, though it quickly vanished in the next instant.

"Just continue with your studies and keep out of harm's way Ronin. My eyes are ever watchful so do not mistake my hospitality for compassion. For if I detect even the slightest hint of maliciousness from you, then you will promptly find yourself fried until you are little more than a pile of ash." Elena emphasized her point by conjuring a few crackling sparks in her hand and dancing them between her fingers like they were coins. This was the second time she had blatantly threatened his life in such a fashion, though her tone in this case was a little bit more casual than before, almost like a tease. Perhaps her words were intended to be partially a joke, but Ronin most definitely did not interpret them that way.

Without another word, Elena walked past him, and he watched as she vanished into another part of the coven. Ronin rolled his eyes annoyedly.

"It's like she's a child, young adult, and an elder all mixed into one person."

A warm and crackling fire hissed pleasantly beside Ronin as he sat in a cushioned chair reading his new books in the privacy of his room. Upon further inspection, the materials Elena had given him turned out to be even more rudimentary than he first thought, as if they were written for children. It provided a kind of welcome, if a little embarrassing, sense of relief. In a strange way, it felt almost like learning how to read all over again. His focus was interrupted though, when there was a knock on his door. Ronin stood up and opened the door to see that Ari had returned, though she now donned her red travel coat and carried a sizable backpack in her hand. She gave Ronin a friendly nod as she stood in front of him.

"Going somewhere?" he asked.

"Indeed. I must head into town to restock our supplies, and as comfortable as I am in the dark, I'd still prefer to get back before nightfall," answered Ari, a soft groan poorly hidden under her breath.

"I see. Wasn't that what you were doing the day you found me in the cave though?"

"It was, however, part of Jey's terms for negotiating with Elena involved taking his chore shifts... for a while. Would you care to join me?" While Ronin did feel a little guilty as he considered that it was mainly his fault that Ari was in such a position in the first place, the idea of going back to a town he had nearly been murdered in just a few days ago was not particularly appealing to him. Still though, Ronin figured it would be best to not so quickly forget his old way of life by residing in the coven day after day. And given that he had slain his hunter, and would be in the company of a powerful witch during the trip, he relented.

"Uh, I suppose I could accompany you," he said.

"Splendid!" cheered Ari as she tossed the empty bag to Ronin. This action, combined with the somewhat coy look she was giving him made it all too clear that his role in her punishment was lost on neither of them.

What Ronin had anticipated would be a pleasant stroll through the woods towards the city, had in reality turned out to be an arduous hike that proved tedious for even an experienced traveler such as himself. The terrain that surrounded the coven was borderline hazardous, being packed full of steep, rocky hills and ledges, as well as a seemingly never-ending swarm of dense vegetation that blocked the view of everything behind it. Clearly people almost never ventured this deep into the woods. Thankfully though, Ari was quite familiar with the area, and guided them through the worst of it. Eventually, they arrived at the long countryside road that ran towards the city.

"So why do we even need to go into town to buy food anyways? Are there truly no spells to conjure or grow it faster?" asked Ronin as their feet pitter pattered along the much more comfortable terrain. Were it not for their present company of each other, the ongoing journey would have been quite lonely, as little aside from the occasional squirrel or bird made itself known across the path, to say nothing for actual travelers.

"We can only ever cast spells from our respective schools, remember? I've read that the life school has access to magic that can cause crops to grow at accelerated rates, though I've never encountered a member of it," said Ari. A warm midday sun progressively beamed down on them brighter as the tree line above began to thin out. Ari closed her eyes and smiled softly, letting its warmth caress her exposed face.

"You know surprisingly, I've always been fond of bright and sunny days like these," said Ari as she took a deep inhale of fresh air. "The night may give me strength, but it's not as if the sun and I are enemies."

"I guess that makes sense... " said Ronin confusedly. "Even so, it's still a little strange. I can't quite say that a supposed rivalry between the sun and a person is a subject I ever would have given much thought to up until a few days ago."

"Understandably so. Many concepts pertaining to magic have little to no direct relevance in the natural world. I have yet to meet one familiar with the arcane arts who is not also an avid philosopher."

"Point taken... and speaking of which... " began Ronin as he stopped in place and turned to face Ari. He glanced down and uncomfortably scratched his neck, feeling embarrassed by what was on his mind.

"Yes?"

"Well, I've been wondering about this for a while now... if magic and witches are real, then does that mean that any other occultish or supernatural stuff is real? You know uh, werewolves, vampires, ghosts... demons perhaps?" Ronin tried his best to sound purely curious as he asked away, but did a poor job of masking the worry in his voice.

"Haha!" Ari laughed with a hand over her mouth. "If any of those things are real, then they definitely haven't decided to introduce themselves to me yet. Don't worry though, if you can no longer rely on ignorance to calm yourself to sleep at night, you can instead use magic," she teased, much to Ronin's dismay.

Ronin and Ari continued to make occasional chit chat as they traveled alone along the road. After a short while longer, they found themselves standing at the top of a slight hill, from which the city they sought came into view. Ari continued walking towards the city, but Ronin turned to his side and paused to take in the scenery. The landscape looked eerily familiar to him; they couldn't be far from where he'd fought with his attacker. Ronin had fled away from the main road and into the dense forestry surrounding it, a route few aside from farmers and herbalists would ever bother to venture down. Given that this had all only happened just a few days ago, it was entirely possible that the man's body was still there. This meant that finding Ronin's lost handcloth would be an easy matter of walking around until the foul scent of decay caught his nose.

He took a single step forward, but found himself freezing involuntarily as his foot left the road and landed on the grass beside it. A part of Ronin wanted to rush back into the woods in search of his lost possession, but that same urge presently felt more like a longing cry than genuine desire. Ronin looked down to see his boot pressing into the dirt. To his side was a prospering, lively, ordinary city, as well as someone willing to guide his hand through it. And ahead was the bleak nothingness of the world, filled with little more than meaningless paths and empty promises. Ronin again found himself wondering if he was dreaming. An unexpected yank of his arm shook Ronin back to attention.

"Hello?!" called out Ari annoyedly as she waved a hand in front of his face. "I've been calling your name for almost a minute now. Is everything alright?" Ronin rubbed his eyes as reality set back in.

"Sorry. I'm fine," he answered while starting to walk towards the city again. "I was just daydreaming." With every step he took, Ronin could feel that same longing cry tugging him back like a distressed child, but he tried to ignore it as best as he could.

As they marched down the hill towards the main gate, Ronin could hear the sounds of chatter and traffic progressively growing louder. He always found himself feeling anxious when moving through large crowds, which was partially why he often traveled through back streets and alleys. He wanted to draw the hood of his cloak, but knew that doing so in public could attract attention, which was the last thing he wanted. Guards of most kingdoms, Rendolyn included, were known to often look at the law through rather obscured lenses, making encountering them an often-precarious situation. And given that Ronin was about as far detached from noble birth as one could ever imagine being, he was well aware that his word and life would carry little meaning if he angered them.

They arrived at the presently open gate, the path through which gave way to a small square that Ronin hadn't seen before. The entry taxes most cities and towns instituted were often rather hefty, a tendency that was confirmed present when Ari reluctantly handed over some coins to the guard posted by the gate. Such a tax was more than enough of an incentive for Ronin to simply opt to hop the walls under cover of darkness most of the time. This area didn't seem quite as busy as the central market, but some degree of traffic and business was more or less constant throughout the day. Many stalls and vendors lined the sides of the square, no doubt looking to capitalize on the impatience of tired and hungry travelers as they first arrived within the city. Ari, however, didn't give any of these salespersons so much as a passing glance as she walked briskly along the road, with Ronin following in tow. She clearly had some specific destination in mind. As they proceeded past the exit of the square into the heart of the town, Ronin took note of a large wooden sign that was hanging prominently above the road: 'Welcome to Meadow's Peak,' it read.

"Huh. So that's what this place is called."

The further they progressed into the city and the closer they got to the market, the busier the activity became. The streets were narrow as well, so much so that Ronin and Ari had to nearly press against each other just to avoid getting separated. Upon arriving in the market itself, Ari guided Ronin into a larger building.

Inside were shelves and tables all packed to the brim with an abundance of products and commodities for nearly any day to day situation Ronin could imagine. Food, alcohol, clothing, tools, basic weapons, and more feasted his eyes, though they were all labeled with prices that caused his heart to skip a beat as he browsed amongst them alongside a handful of other customers.

"Ah! Greetings Ariana. I never reckoned I'd see you back so soon," announced a voice from a figure Ronin saw emerging from a back room. A large, hefty looking man with short messy hair and a deep voice strolled across the shop and behind the counter where purchases were made. Ari smiled cheerfully at the man as she walked over to him.

"Good day Bertram. I can't say I'm all too proud to be back like this, but it's good to see you at least," said Ari embarrassedly. Ronin stood next to one of the nearby tables, feigning interest in a collection of travel pouches as he listened in on their conversation. Ari and the shopkeeper she called Bertram seemed genuinely happy to see each other, though Ronin assumed they were simply exchanging business pleasantries. This assumption, though, was shot down almost immediately when Ronin heard a sudden fit of jovial laughter from the man as he reached forward to pat Ari's head as if she were his daughter.

"Aye, you as well lass. Spill the story already though, what happened with the last supply shipment I gave you?" asked Bertram a little too excitedly.

"Ah... well... I got into a bit of an accident by the Wailing River on my way back home. Let's just say those preserved fish of yours are the ones on their way back home now, along with everything else." Bertram started snickering at Ari's expense as he listened to her dodgy explanation, only stopping when she started to scowl at him.

"My apologies sweetheart," he said, even though he was still smiling. "What kind of accident was it though? Are you alright?"

"Just a slip up. I'm fine," Ari answered. Ronin could hear the change in her tone after Bertram pushed her for more information. Oddly enough, her voice now lacked a degree of the cheerfulness he had become used to, and before the shopkeeper could get another word in, she changed the subject.

"I'm here to pick up another resupply, however it will need to be somewhat larger than usual this time, say a thirty three percent increase?" requested Ari as she gestured to her side at Ronin.

"I see. And who might this be?" asked Bertram as Ronin looked up from the wares and walked over to them.

"A longtime friend of mine visiting from afar," answered Ari.

"My name is Ronin. It's a pleasure to meet you sir."

"Likewise, lad," replied Bertram as he reached over and gave a handshake so firm that Ronin worried he may get dragged back over the counter. "For your sake I hope your friendship with Ariana here is just that. A girl such as herself could run your pockets dry in a matter of hours with her extravagance if your chivalry were to get the best of you," joked Bertram. Ronin chuckled somewhat awkwardly, but stopped shortly as he caught a glance at Ari out of the corner of his eye. Bertram's words seemed to strike her unexpectedly. A mild twitch and sharp blink of her eyes once again left her cheerful persona betrayed, and Ronin worried that he and Bertram had offended her.

"Anyways," continued Bertram. "Supply bundles have admittedly been selling fast in preparation for the coming winter, though I should still have what you require, so long as our usual arrangements are scaled appropriately?"

"Of course," said Ari plainly.

"Excellent! Wait here a moment then," Bertram told them before returning to the back room.

"What sort of special arrangements would you have with a shopkeeper?" asked Ronin out of curiosity.

"Bertram opened this store when I was a little girl, and I've been a customer ever since. I slide him a little extra coin under the table, and in return he provides us with the best provisions he has, alongside a promise to not document the transaction. It may seem odd, but it's just another one of the many tiresome safety precautions Elena enforces," replied Ari quietly.

"Magic, hiding in the woods, and now shady business practices now. You really are something out of a fairytale," whispered Ronin to Ari's amusement.

A moment later Bertram re-emerged from the storage room, carrying a large basket of supplies beneath his arm. He placed it down on the counter in front of Ronin and Ari, and Ronin promptly began to stuff all of it into the backpack Ari had given him while she shuffled around with her coin purse.

"I believe this should cover everything," said Ari as she slid several large silver coins across the counter.

"I'm certain of it," replied Bertram as he took the coins without even bothering to check them. "Do be more careful with this shipment though you two. I wasn't joking when I said they're selling fast. Crime and smuggling have been on the rise lately, and the priests worry our sins may bring about an especially harsh winter soon enough."

"And you're really inclined to believe them?" asked Ari with a skeptic smirk.

"Er, well, can't be too careful now, can you?"

"Indeed," answered Ronin. While the forebodings of priests meant nothing to him, he still winced slightly as he recalled the many harsh winters he had endured over the years, during which the pity of strangers trying to do their good deed for the day had been his most reliable tool for survival. At the same time though, he relaxed as he considered how the coven would provide guaranteed shelter this season, a luxury he hadn't known for several years.

After thanking Bertram for the sale and bidding him farewell, Ari and Ronin stepped back outside into the bustling market. Ronin grunted softly as the supplies he carried turned out to be a little heavier than he anticipated.

"Your role as my travel servant would appear far more convincing if you carried our goods more sturdily," teased Ari.

"Travel servant? I thought I was your friend from afar?"

"To the people I introduce you to you are. But you can't expect me to explain such to all the folk we pass on the streets." Ronin felt a little flustered by her banter, and wanted to retaliate, but could only think to roll his eyes before she turned away and guided him elsewhere. He frustratingly knew that he would only be able to come up with a proper comeback after having reviewed the exchange numerous times in his head.

Their journey through Meadow's Peak persisted for some time. After a while, the streets grew wider and less congested as they crossed into another district. The buildings around them were larger than average, as well as cleaner and more decorative. The further they walked, the more Ronin began to anxiously shoot his gaze back and forth and all around, as if he were being beckoned to from every direction. Eventually, he realized where they were.

"Why are we going through the upper-class district?" he asked worrisomely.

"This is simply the way to get to our next stop. Is something the matter?" Ari didn't seem to understand why he was on edge. Ari's clothes were of exceptional quality, and her demeanor helped her fit in perfectly. Ronin on the other hand, despite wearing the equally fine attire he had received from her, still felt that he stood out like a sore thumb.

"I suppose not for now... however people like me are not usually welcomed with open arms in places like this."

"Sounds like nothing more than another reason to play up your servant persona," replied Ari. Ronin scowled at her from outside her view; he still didn't have a comeback. He tried his best to stand up straight and carry their supplies with a bit more dignity, much to his frustration.

The road ahead soon gave way to a fork, with one path branching off further into the district, and the other quickly leading up to a large wooden gate bearing a family seal of a large willow tree. Ronin was surprised when Ari turned away from the main road and walked up to the gate. He watched her grasp one of its large handles and push it open so carefree as if she were entering her own home. In the near distance, beyond a walkway and garden nearly overgrown with brightly colored flowers and other vegetation, sat an estate more glamorous than any home Ronin had seen before, even in paintings.

"Perhaps I should wait for you here... " suggested Ronin, whose knees shook at the prospect of entering the property.

"Why would you do that? Are you afraid the more exotic plants might poison you?" joked Ari.

"The plants themselves, no. Whatever powerful lord you're in such a rush to deal with, maybe."

"The lady of this house is a great friend of mine who would never harm a blade of grass, much less a person."

"Okay but-" began Ronin before being cut off as Ari grabbed him by the arm and pulled him through the gate.

"Stop worrying so much. If you were fascinated by the books in the coven then I promise you won't want to miss our business here."

The walkway towards the front door of the estate was short, or at least it would have been were it not for the many twists and turns the path took around various flower beds, fish ponds, and vegetable patches. The property was certainly luxurious, yet the ambiance instilled a quaint and humble sensation as well that felt a little contradictory to Ronin. The front entrance to the building rested beneath a high balcony and on top of a small stone patio. When the two of them arrived at the door, Ari quickly banged her fist against it sort of rudely. Silence followed for a long moment, being interrupted by nothing more than the sounds of running water from a nearby stream.

"Are you sure we don't need an appointment?" asked Ronin with complete seriousness.

"We don't. The lady of this house lives alone, but if she had a steward, I'd sooner blast this door open than deal with them." Ronin was about to ask if Ari was joking or not, but stopped as he heard a soft clicking sound, and watched as the door in front of them was slowly pulled open. Standing inside a dimly lit hallway was an older woman, perhaps ten years their senior. She looked fittingly aristocratic, with well-kept brown hair and a finely tailored purple dress covering her from chest to toe. When she glanced at the both of them, Ari in particular, standing on her porch, she gave a sort of exasperated sigh that Ronin would expect from a disappointed mentor.

"Let me guess... " she began with a quiet yet stern voice. "Little Jeremiah wasted my brews in yet another botched experiment?"

Ari laughed at the woman's assumption.

"I'm afraid not, however much I may wish that were the case. The loss of your potions this time is my own fault," she said.

"I see... " replied the woman skeptically. "That's rather uncharacteristic of you. How exactly did such a mistake occur?"

"A travel accident," answered Ari quickly, and with much the same tone she had responded to Bertram with.

"A travel accident you say... " said the woman after a pause for speculation. "And just a random one at that? I seem to recall you looking rather pale during your previous visit." The woman's words trailed off her tongue in a noticeably accusatory tone whenever she finished speaking.

"Do all not look pale in the eyes of one who lives amongst a grounded rainbow of flora?" retorted Ari. The woman glared at Ari, as if to make her disapproval known for certain, before relenting. Ari glared right back at her, but in the following moment, they both seemed to force a smile across their faces as they each stepped forward and embraced each other in a tight hug.

"I suppose I at least get to see you again for now, Ariana," said the woman

"Likewise, Sorem."

When they pulled away from each other, the woman known as Sorem turned to face Ronin. "I'm honored to meet you," she said with a respectful bow of her head.

"Oh, um... the honor is all mine," stuttered Ronin as he returned the gesture. He felt wholly shocked and embarrassed that such a wealthy noblewoman would bow to him, especially given that she was noticeably older than he was.

"Coming face to face with a new witch is a rare but most welcome occurrence these days. Please, come in and make yourselves at home," said Sorem as she stepped out of their way and held the door open wide. Ari strolled right inside, with Ronin following more hesitantly.

"H-how did you know that about me?" he asked as he passed her.

"If Ariana here has the confidence to bring you to my home unannounced, then you certainly must be a magic wielder yourself, or at least one fully acquainted with their existence."

Much like outdoors, the inside of Sorem's estate also teemed with various kinds of plant life. Some were ordinary like cherry blossoms and sunflowers, but others were downright unrecognizable to Ronin, possessing thick and twisting limb-like stems with thinner strands draping over them like hair. The only real difference he could point out between the inside and the outside were the four walls and roof that currently surround them. Sorem led Ari and Ronin into a large and cozy living room, where Ronin assumed she and Ari would talk business of some kind. Just as he was about to take a seat though, Sorem approached a fireplace across the room, and pulled tightly on a small stone statuette atop it. The figure dropped forward like a lever, and suddenly a loud grinding sound of rock and stone filled Ronin's ears as a slab on the floor beneath the fireplace retracted backwards, revealing a narrow staircase leading into an otherwise secret basement.

The noise was stunning enough to make Ronin gasp, and he had to brace himself against the back of a chair to avoid falling. Ari chuckled at his reaction.

"After you," said Sorem while gesturing down the steps. Ronin stepped past her, but paused as he stared down the dark staircase. The claustrophobic and dusty interior actually bore an uncanny resemblance to the kinds of places he was most familiar with, but that certainly didn't make Ronin feel more comfortable. "Something the matter?" asked Sorem.

"Not really... I've just seen a handful of dungeons before," answered Ronin.

"Haha! It takes far more than a few iron bars and stones to imprison powerful witches," joked Sorem as she urged him down the steps. When they arrived at the bottom, Ronin's eyes went wide as he saw what looked like an elaborate laboratory hidden beneath the estate. Various glass beakers, test tubes, and pipes stood and winded throughout the room, most of them filled with bizarre, multicolored substances that looked like juice mixed with sludge. Papers, tools, and more all lay cluttered across a handful of tables and desks, as well as a large oven that resided in the corner of the room.

To Ronin's still somewhat ignorant mind, this basement seemed just as guilty of witchcraft as anything he had seen from Ari, Elena, or Jey. He scanned the room until his eyes caught the sight of Sorem smiling with pride at his clear amazement.

"What is all this?" he asked while reaching out to touch one of one the glass containers.

"It's obvious is it not?" questioned Ari as she slapped his hand away from the devices. "Sorem here is what we may refer to as a... high profile botanist and alchemist...?" summarized Ari as she looked to Sorem for approval, who shrugged and chuckled at her.

"I see... " replied the still confused Ronin. "But what in the world does that have to do with your magic?" he asked Sorem.

"You seem to be mistaken, Ronin," she answered as she strolled over to one of the desks and began fumbling through a stack of papers. "I do not wield such power for myself. I merely provide those who do with the means to further enhance and hone their abilities."

"Certain plants carry properties that, when brewed into potions, can augment our spell casting power. And conversely, there are many spells that can be used to alter or strengthen the properties of said potions," chimed in Ari.

"Aye. However, all of this ultimately comes down to the quality of the initial brew, and when you're the best potion specialist on this half of Rendolyn, witches tend to pay a fairly steep price. It's a carefully guarded secret my ancestors found out many generations ago," teased Sorem. As he listened to their words, Ronin continued to stare curiously at the many vials and tubes in front of him. The liquids inside that he presumed were for the potions looked anything but tasty or thirst quenching, though at the same time he couldn't resist being allured to their supposed potential.

"These potions of yours... could they perhaps help me..."

"Don't get overly excited," said Ari, cutting him off. "Potions can only ever empower our abilities after the fact. They can bolster the effects of our magic, but they cannot cast the spells for us, so to speak." Ronin felt a wave of disappointment wash over him, but like any single wave, it was soon gone. He never raised his expectations all that high.

"Aha!" cheered Sorem as she yanked a piece of paper out from the pile. "I've found your order form, Ariana."

"And in as timely a fashion as always," snarked Ari.

"I would ask you to mind your tone, young lady. I'm sure your master would not appreciate your treating her business partner so poorly."

"As if you'd ever muster up the energy to contact her." The two of them laughed as Sorem gathered a handful of herbs and began the process of converting their resources into various concoctions.

Time ticked by as Sorem churned out one mixture after another, which she then poured into small glass bottles that she passed over to Ronin. He examined each one closely before carefully placing them inside his increasingly heavy backpack. There was an enormous variety amongst all of the potions. Some were watery and red like blood, while others were thicker and multicolored, almost like a paste or jam.

"These potions seem nigh otherworldly. It can't be safe to sell them," said Ronin. Sorem chuckled bashfully through her hand at his confusion.

"Concerned for us, are you? Worry not; your interpretation is backwards," she began. "I don't mean to frighten you Ronin, but you yourself are at far greater risk by coming here than I am. If a stranger on the street is so much as suspected of dabbling in fabled witchcraft, then they will surely be swiped away as quickly as possible. However, a noble who carries influence and wealth? It's far more difficult to expose, let alone remove them, don't you agree?"

"Ah, of course..." Ronin laughed in self-pity at her explanation, feeling stupid that he of all people didn't arrive at such a conclusion. Sorem handed him the final potion, and he watched as Ari fished out most of what remained in her coin purse that at this point had ceased its audible jingling. She and Sorem then sat beside each other and shared some more banter and chit chat afterwards, which left Ronin standing impatiently as he waited for the two women to finish their conversation so he and Ari could leave.

It was only then that Ronin realized that this time, Ari didn't introduce him to Sorem as her friend from afar. She also spoke of magic so leisurely, like how bar friends would chat about horse races or cock fights. There was no need for discretion amongst the three of them. Here, they were all just whoever they were supposed to be, whatever that even meant. A witch, an alchemist, and... someone else. Ronin suddenly heard them calling him over, and looked to see Sorem offering him a chair. Right now, all he felt like was a guest.

Chapter Four
What I Brought with Me

The day continued on, and the air began to chill slightly as the sun surpassed its midday peak. A soft breeze blew clusters of autumn leaves down across the cobblestone streets to be trampled beneath horses and pedestrians. As their shopping spree came to a close, Ronin and Ari could feel the fatigue of their several hours of walking around begin to overcome them.

"We have everything I needed to purchase now. Care for a bit of rest before heading back home?" asked Ari.

"O-oh um, sure," stuttered Ronin.

"Splendid! The local tavern has a splendid atmosphere; you'll love it." Ari then proceeded to guide Ronin across the market square towards a large wooden building that seemed to constantly have a handful of people either entering or leaving.

Most of the structures in Meadow's Peak were made out of a combination of simple stone and plank wood, though the quality of which varied greatly depending on what district the building was in, and how recently it was made. The tavern, fittingly named 'The Road Through Time,' as Ronin read on a sign above the front door, looked to be a hybrid of the structure of the rest of the city, as if it were under constant renovation. For each newly crafted plank of wood that held up its foundation, there was an equally withered and faded board somewhere else. The distinction was so jarring in some areas that Ronin found himself wondering if someone was progressively constructing an identical tavern from the old materials someplace else. Ronin felt a little uneasy as he and Ari approached the front door of the building, a sensation that quickly grew when Ari casually pushed the door open. The inside of the place was so vibrant and lively that it overloaded Ronin's senses right away. A warm fire from a large hearth struck down any chills that tried to creep in through the doorway, while the potent aromas of hot food and fine drink filled his nostrils. The chaotic noise from patrons echoed throughout the building like a never-ending musical of cheers and laughs.

They made it not five steps past the doorway before a young barmaid carrying a tray of drinks over her shoulder spotted them, and approached with a joyful smile.

"Ari! Welcome back!" greeted the short brunette-haired girl with a wave of her hand that clumsily made her nearly drop the tray she carried. She gasped loudly as Ari pounced forward to help keep her steady.

"I can't imagine how you have been able to keep your job like this, Lucina. Is it even worth it to keep reminding you to be careful?"

"Aha... I suppose not. I'm getting by though, that much I can promise." The girl's face was red with embarrassment. "Anyways... " she continued. "I take it you'd like a table?"

"That would be quite nice," answered Ari. Lucina turned to continue on into the main dining room of the tavern, and motioned for them to follow.

"You'll have to tell me all about him sometime," she whispered to Ari while making a painfully indiscreet gesture towards Ronin.

"Oh, it's not a story you would believe," replied Ari, who made no effort whatsoever to keep her voice down in front of Ronin.

Lucina led them to a cozy booth for two that was nuzzled away in a small corner of the room, which provided some modest privacy.

"Here we are. What can I get you then?"

"I'll have my usual, as well as a sharing size portion of wheat bread with butter and honey on the side," answered Ari.

"And for you sir?" asked Lucina as she turned to Ronin.

"N-nothing for me. Thank you," he answered timidly. Ronin then glanced down at his hands and picked at his fingernails for a few seconds, until he eventually noticed the awkward silence that had arisen. He slowly glanced back up to see the critical expressions of the two girls bearing down on him like vultures. "Aha... ale then. Thank you..." Ronin smiled embarrassedly. He compromised to order something he assumed would be on the cheaper side of the menu. Lucina smiled and nodded at them both before departing.

"You are aware that I will be paying, aren't you? Order whatever you like and consider it my thanks for accompanying me today," said Ari with a soft giggle.

"I see." Ronin had genuinely not picked up on her offer. "I'm fine though. Truth be told, I wouldn't really know what else to order anyways."

"Not much of a drinker, are you?"

"No. At least not from places like this." Ronin took a slow glance, around the open and lively room, his expression looking like that of a lost child.

"Hmm... " muttered Ari as she toyed with her hair.

"Yes?"

"You know I may be the 'witch,' here, but you yourself are no less an enigma, oh mysterious Ronin," Ari said in a whisper.

"What's that supposed to mean? People usually find my existence pretty believable, at least once they actually notice me," replied Ronin as he awkwardly tried to avoid Ari's curious gaze.

"All I'm saying is that we've known each for several days and will be living together for the foreseeable future. It would make sense for us to learn a bit more about each other, don't you agree?"

"I suppose so," answered Ronin a little reluctantly. "I've not much to tell though. I have no exciting stories or remarkable interests."

"Let's start simple then. Where are you from?" Ronin was slow to respond to her question as he thought of how to answer. "Have I in fact not chosen a simple opening question?"

"My apologies, that's a difficult question to answer for no reason other than that well, there is no real answer." His words clearly confused Ari.

"Hmm, surely you don't mean to insinuate that you simply crawled out of a river one day?"

"I suppose that could be the case," said Ronin only half-jokingly. "I've never known anything about my true home or family. I grew up at an orphanage in Swampburg, a faraway town by the eastern coast. The caretakers told me that I was just dropped off as a baby one day, no paperwork or anything. That's all I have ever known of where I'm from so to speak."

As he spoke, Ronin's tone gradually became more and more longing, though not for the warm comforts of the home he never had. The more he recounted his story, the more he thought back to his tiresome quest for answers about his past. It felt like an itch that stubbornly refused to leave whether it was scratched or ignored. He sighed in frustration, and futilely attempted to force such intrusive thoughts out of his head.

"I was right then; you hold many surprises. My apologies though, I didn't intend to raise a sensitive subject," said Ari.

"Oh, don't worry. I've long since come to terms with who I am... "

"I see... Do continue then. Surely your tale doesn't end there."

"Hm. Well, I only stayed at that first orphanage until about my seventh winter. From there it closed down for reasons I never learned, and I was bounced around from orphanage to orphanage across many different towns and regions. I don't think adoption is a particularly desirable idea for most folk these days. That or...never mind. When

I was around fourteen years old, I was sent off on my own. I've spent the last couple of years roaming the streets and roads as I please, more or less," finished Ronin.

"Wow, you must have done your fair share of traveling then. I'm impressed, though I struggle to fathom how you've gotten by."

"Aha... " chuckled Ronin. "I've used many different means to do so, though I will admit that some of them have been less than admirable at times... "

"Oh my, you're a mysterious rogue then?" I find myself all the more interested now," replied Ari with a coy grin. "Still though, it does sound like a difficult life."

"I guess. It's hard to say though, seeing as how I've never known anything else." Ronin shrugged.

"Hm, well I hope that soon enough you will feel differently."

"Huh? What do you mean?" asked Ronin. Ari didn't answer right away though. She simply stared at him from across the table with a knowing smile, as if she were beckoning him to answer himself. Ronin felt his face go slightly red, and he knew what she'd meant.

He wanted to say something back to Ari, something to express his gratitude for everything she'd done for him. Even a simple 'thank you,' would have sufficed, but in the moment, he felt as if he had somehow managed to unlearn his native language. His throat grew dry, his mind blank, but fortunately albeit also a little disappointingly, his train of thought was suddenly interrupted by the sounds of several tankards and plates clunking down onto the table in front of them.

"Here you are. Let me know if you need anything else!" said Lucina as she gave them a slight bow of her head before heading off to attend to some other customers. Ari thanked her politely before cupping her drink between her hands and taking a long, savory sip of wine.

"Ah, two years I've been drinking here now, and the taste is just as delectable as it was the very time." She motioned for Ronin to drink with her. Ronin grabbed his tankard by the handle and raised it to his lips. He took a quick whiff of its scent. The ale smelled far fresher than what he was familiar with, giving him the impression that it was brewed in house. He took a small sip and savored its sweet and fruity taste, before reaching with his other hand to take a piece of bread and spread some butter on it. It was soft, warm, and simply delicious. Far better than the usual food he either scavenged for himself or purchased from cheap street vendors in the poorer districts of towns, even if it was still just bread. He couldn't help but grin softly as he continued to eat and drink.

"Mm, quite good right?" chimed in Ari with her own mouth full.

"Certainly so." Ronin glanced back up. "You really are quite fond of this city, perhaps more so than you cared to let on at first?" Ari responded with a smirk and a wink.

"I am," she said, her lips forming a pleasant yet seemingly longing smile. "It's quite active and high spirited here year-round, even during the winter to an extent. Do not misunderstand me, I truly love my home, and Elena and Jey are like family to me, but all of these charades we play, the hiding in the woods, the fake personas, the overly precautious way we carry ourselves when doing everything from buying food to taking a leisurely woodland stroll... it all becomes rather tiring."

"I wish I could relate more," said Ronin. "If it's any consolation though, you aren't missing much. Most towns and cities rarely look or feel any different from one another, and Meadow's Peak here is among the nicer ones."

"Aye, perhaps that is true, but can you really say so yourself?"

"Huh?"

"Don't think your demeanor has gone unnoticed. That is to say the way you carry yourself with your eyes down wherever we go. Can you sincerely tell me that in all your travels you've gazed upon such places through a clear lens?" Ronin stuttered to himself for a moment, feeling flustered by her keen perception and sudden accusation.

"Ah well, I suppose I never have been much for tourism," he said rather meekly, which earned him a satisfied smirk from Ari.

"The market here is quite expansive, as I'm sure you saw. Since Meadow's Peak is right along the main road from the border of Rendolyn to the capital, many traders from dozens of lands pass through here. It's like having a whole chunk of world right before you, or well, at least a little taste of it."

"I know nothing of exotic goods, but I did happen to spot a lot of more regional merchandise. Rare pelts from the north, salt from the coast; all things I saw more of when I was bouncing around the kingdom." Ari let out a soft sigh as she spoke.

"Ah, so it would seem you have paid at least some attention to the places you have visited." Her further teasing began to irk Ronin a bit.

"I pay most attention to that which can benefit me, which just so happens to be a region's valuable commodities most of the time. It's not a habit I am proud of, but one I live by out of necessity given I've no one to look after me. In contrast, your home may not have much in the way of diversity, but for all the curiosity you may have of places afar, can you sincerely tell me that you would be willing to forfeit the luxuries of a roof over your head and familiar faces to wake up to?"

Ronin sat back in his booth, arms crossed and with a smirk of his own on his lips as he waited for Ari's response, but found himself caught off guard as she said nothing right away. She instead stared at him for a moment, her face plain and unmoving. As the moment persisted, Ronin began to feel more and more uncomfortable, and started to worry that he had hurt her feelings. Just as he was about to give in and apologize though, Ari suddenly burst into a fit of laughter.

"Aha! I'll admit that I am pleasantly surprised to see you act so assertive for a change. Though if you knew me just a tad bit better, you'd be well aware that I never settle," she said softly, and with an alluring smile that made Ronin jolt in place ever so slightly. "I would not so lightly give up such things that I am truly grateful for, nor would I ever abandon my own ambitions out of complacency. I simply intend to have the best of both worlds one day." Ronin stumbled a bit, feeling taken aback by her confidence.

"I find that hard to imagine unless you and your friends decide to become a traveling band of gypsies. Have you any plans for accomplishing this?" he asked doubtfully as he raised his drink for another sip. Ari opened her mouth to answer, but Ronin heard nothing other than a sudden and obnoxious laughter that interrupted their conversation.

"That certainly is the question at hand, is it not?" came a raspy voice. Ronin and Ari glanced to their sides to see a strange young man slowly approaching them from another table, though Ronin didn't look for long. He gagged a bit, and had to seal his lips shut as best as he could to avoid spitting his drink all over Ari and the table. His skin was crawling, but he took a discreetly deep breath and managed to steady himself. On the inside though, Ronin was in such a state of disbelief that his nerves shook like a mountain experiencing an avalanche. The strange man stood tall, and donned a suit of light leather armor beneath a dark green travel cloak. It was the exact same uniform that Ronin's would be murderer from a few days ago had been wearing.

The man's hood was drawn back, revealing long strands of dirty blonde hair that dangled around a toothy grin.

"You're wasting your time, friend," he said. "As are you, Ariana. I still can't bring myself to understand why anyone would ever be so rejectful of the solution to their desires. Especially when it is staring at them in the face so literally." He eyed Ari from above, his fingers pitter pattering over the table. Ari sighed heavily, her head collapsing into a hand she held upright as she rolled her eyes in clear frustration.

"As I've said before, Zane..." Ari made no attempt to hide her disdain for the man as she spoke his name. "Neither my explanation nor your inability to comprehend it are surprising. You are simply too short sighted to realize that there are people in this world with values that don't match your own." She spoke with only one eye fixed upon the man she called Zane, refusing to acknowledge him so much as to turn and face him in conversation.

"Perhaps, but we are not speaking of other people's values, are we now?" asked Zane while he reached behind himself to steal a chair from another table before taking a seat beside Ari and Ronin. "Why don't you reevaluate my offer here, seeing as how you've conveniently just recited your own wants. I can give you whatever you please, excitement, adventure, comfort, as well company and no shortage of luxury on the road. Week after week I see you toiling away through these same tired streets and buildings, and for what purpose? To return home to buy more time to lurk about until the cycle must repeat itself?" His words slithered off the tongue like a snake over grass, so much so that Ronin wondered if the man's breath alone could be enough to butcher one of weaker will. "Such a life is not at all befitting of a maiden of your impeccably rare beauty," he said as he slowly slid his hand across the table to hers.

Ari promptly scowled and slapped his hand away. She refused to glorify his advances with any more of a response. Evidently, this conversation had already been resolved in her eyes.

"Ah... how unfortunate. And here I was just trying to be a gentleman." Zane seemed to vocally concede, but gave no indication that he planned on leaving her alone. Ronin felt himself shaking ever so slightly in his seat as his frustration started to rise. Ari was obviously bothered by Zane even if she seemed to take him about as seriously as a buzzing insect. A part of Ronin wanted to do something to try and get rid of him, but at the same time, he figured it would be safest to avoid drawing attention to himself. However, Ronin's patience ran short almost as soon as Zane started to relax in his seat, and called out to a barmaid to order a drink for himself.

"She said she's not interested. And we were trying to enjoy a nice lunch," said Ronin. As soon as he spoke, Zane, perhaps a little too readily, shot his gaze in Ronin's direction with the speed and precision of a wolf hearing a branch snap behind it.

"And who might you be?" Zane asked, a disturbing calmness lingering about his voice.

"He is-" began Ari before Zane cut her off.

"Hold on Ariana, don't be so ill-mannered. I know his type. A long cloak - that I must admit is rather fashionable - combined with a face still unfamiliar to me despite my many recent visits to this tavern. A traveler no doubt, and one who has just recently arrived in town nonetheless. Surely someone who is capable of braving the long and dangerous paths of the wilderness seemingly by his lonesome can answer his own name."

Ronin said nothing more to Zane at first, and instead stared ahead at Ari with a worried expression, his eyes begging her not to answer or even say anything at all to Zane for the matter. Zane spoke with the same kind of wholly exaggerated arrogance Ronin had learned to expect from country road bandits who considered themselves kings in rulership of the vast plains of nothingness they so cowardly awaited their traveling prey in. And if it were not for Ronin's worry that concealed beneath Zane's cloak was yet another ensemble of knight worthy weaponry, he would've accused Zane of such to his face.

"We've no business with each other, so my name is of no importance. Now if you'd be so kind as to leave us in peace... "

"Merciful lord," Zane snarked. He seemed to take Ronin with as little seriousness as Ronin wished he could take Zane for. "How can you in good faith imply that I am the one being rude when I am simply trying to acquaint myself with the both of you, and yet neither of you will even give me the courtesy of looking at my face as I speak." Zane leaned slightly closer to Ronin, as if to assert himself. Ronin only dismissed him further by raising his own hood. Zane waited quietly for a couple of seconds, then out of nowhere shot his hand towards Ronin's hood in an attempt to pull it down. Ronin's reflexes were too quick however, and he intercepted Zane's hand with his own, grabbing him by the wrist before giving it a harsh yank that made Zane stumble to the side and nearly fall out of his seat.

As all of this transpired, Ronin noticed that the brief scuffle had caused something to fall out of the part of Zane's cloak around his neck. A small, pointed object attached to a necklace now dangled towards the ground. It looked like a lonesome star, made of a smooth, clear material that encapsulated a mysteriously bright yet fading white glow. Ronin winced slightly in pain as he stared at the puzzling object. A sickly feeling had suddenly overtaken him. He released Zane's wrist, and promptly returned to his idle position in his seat, still refusing to even slightly turn in Zane's direction.

"Why you..." snapped Zane, his jovial and collected persona having completely evaporated. He shot up from his seat aggressively, knocking his chair to the ground with a loud crash in the process. He reached into his cloak as if to draw a weapon, but paused as the rest of the tavern went silent. He turned around and quickly surveyed the building to find that all eyes were now resting on him. Zane let out a low growl before calming himself and turning back to Ari and Ronin.

"I'll take my leave then," he said, his temper having vanished just as quickly as it had appeared. He turned to leave, but stopped briefly to offer a parting message over his shoulder to Ronin. "A word of advice though, from one traveler to another. It is not the slowest, but rather the most stubborn of horses that impede one's journey the most. And I get the impression that you can ill afford to be dragged down much further." On that note, Zane departed off, disappearing out the front door of the tavern and into the clustered crowds outside.

After watching Zane leave, taking the interests of the rest of the tavern with him, Ronin breathed a heavy sigh of relief. He still felt a lingering ache in his throat as well as the rest of his body, but overall, the sickly feeling he'd experienced was gone now, much to his confusion. Fortunately, Zane didn't seem to recognize Ronin the same way his presumed associate had, which gave Ronin hope that maybe his attacker had been working independently at that time. He then turned his attention back to Ari, who was holding her face tightly in both hands as she groaned repeatedly.

"You seem to be quite popular around here."

"Aye, though it's usually far from such a nuisance. How I wish he could be one of the simple boys who offers me no more than a tasty drink or a pleasant stroll."

"I'm sure if you asked, he'd do just that, provided you're willing to receive and return far more in addition. I need to know though, who is he?"

"I'm afraid, but also thankful that I don't know much about him," answered Ari confusedly. "As far as I can tell, Zane is just some fortune craving grunt who relentlessly badgers me every time we cross paths."

"That does sound awfully irritating, but surely you must know some more, no?" persisted Ronin.

"I don't exactly hunt him down for conversation every time I stroll through town," excused Ari. "Why is this so important?" Ronin hesitated to answer at first, feeling unsure of how honest he wanted to be with her. His decision was soon made much easier though, when they were interrupted by Lucina again.

"Are you two okay? I was just a second away from fetching the guards," said the barmaid, her voice filled with worry. Ari was about to say something back, but Ronin cut her off by quickly reaching into his pocket and sliding a silver coin across the table to Lucina.

"No games," he said strictly. "I want all the information you have on this Zane person." Lucina looked at the coin Ronin had offered her with wide eyes. Being a tavern waitress, she could certainly be no stranger to bartering off local gossip and information. That one coin in fact managed to single handedly take up a considerable sum of Ronin's savings, but he figured that the nature of what he was asking for combined with reduced expenses via staying at the coven would make the investment worthwhile.

"Well... " began Lucina with a nonchalant shrug as she pocketed the coin. "Zane is the leader of a traveling band of miscreants; the Darkwood Hunters they call themselves. Their rambunctious and raunchy behavior has given them a reputation akin to that of a brigand group, but as much as I and many others would hate to admit, their success as bounty hunters is undeniable. At least if Zane's boastful claims are to be believed," she said somewhat doubtfully. Ronin flinched anxiously, wishing he could match her disbelief, but Zane's expensive gear and boastful arrogance were both certainly in line with his supposed status. "They bounce around the kingdom wherever new contracts appear, but Zane is known for only ever accepting the highest paying, and typically most dangerous bounties. And seeing as how he is still alive now as we speak, that must mean he has witnessed his fair share of success somehow. He and his men have been working on a contract in the region around Meadow's Peak for some time now, but I'm afraid that's all I can at least as far as confirmed information is concerned."

"And what about unconfirmed information?" asked Ronin.

"Hmm... " muttered Lucina. "As I'm sure you can imagine, a band of infamous bounty hunters strolling in all of a sudden has quickly become the talk of the town. There are a lot of rumors being passed around; most pertain to the nature of the bounty, but others are a bit more... characterized."

"As you saw, Zane is fairly young. He's also relatively new to the bounty hunting scene; none of the other freelancers that have visited here in the meantime had heard of him until a couple of years ago, yet in this time he has managed to muster up a formidable crew and complete numerous high stakes contracts that only veterans ever go for."

"Surely you must have more to say than praises of his success," said Ronin annoyedly.

"His success is unprecedented. People suspect he has a backer, and one with a lot of wealth and power at that." Ronin groaned, and held his face tight in one hand. He was beginning to feel sick again, but this time it was mostly in his stomach.

"That's absurd," interjected Ari. "Surely his feats are exaggerated. Who in the world would care to so heavily support some random boy's delusions of adventure?"

"I wish I could say... " answered Lucina apologetically. Upon hearing her words, Ronin promptly fished another coin out of his pocket and slid it across the table again, much to the bewilderment of his present company. Lucina blushed and pushed the coin back towards Ronin.

"I assure you that I know nothing more."

"Er... very well then. Thank you for your help," replied Ronin who was also feeling embarrassed by his own brashness.

Lucina nodded to him and Ari before returning to her duties.

"You know, I'm starting to feel that the more I learn about you, the less I actually get to know you, Ronin," said Ari somewhat bluntly. "Are you alright?" Such a seemingly simple question was once again anything but that for Ronin. His mind was split in such a way that his thoughts seemed to overlap like battle lines in the thick of the fray. On one side, Ronin considered that Zane's accomplice had certainly been searching for him specifically, and that he was a member of an esteemed bounty hunter group, which could only mean one thing. But why? Ronin wondered so dreadfully. It had been years since he'd stolen anything more than spare crumbs or coins, not exactly the stuff worth hiring a bounty hunter over, even if the contractor was the most egotistical nobleman in all of Rendolyn.

Whatever the reason was though, Ronin had no interest in investigating. Whenever he drew the ire of guards, merchants, or farmhands, Ronin was confident he could evade them just as easily as a bird could evade a wolf. But that hunter was a professional, and Ronin knew that he only won by exploiting the man's overconfidence. Ronin wanted to flee again, and he would have done so without hesitation were it not for the other aspect of his predicament: he wasn't alone this time.

When Ronin looked at Ari, the concern on her face was clear as day. It made a part of him want to explain everything to her, but he hesitated. If Ari knew the truth about the danger surrounding Ronin, how would she react? Would she be afraid of him? Abandon him and flee herself? After all of the kindness she'd shown him, each of these scenarios that painted Ari as yet another person who wanted nothing to do with him terrified Ronin to his core, and he couldn't bring himself to be honest with her. Guilt squeezed and nearly popped Ronin's heart like a rotted piece of fruit as he realized how selfish he was being. But if he could simply return to the coven and lay low through the upcoming winter, then how could anyone be harmed? That was the lone excuse Ronin desperately used to try and distract himself from all other possibilities.

"I... I'm fine," Ronin finally answered. "I just worry that Zane will be a bother for the foreseeable future. I wouldn't fear him though, I know his type even better than he claims to know mine. He may be full of confident talk but I doubt he'd bother to go after someone without a bounty unless you were unlucky enough to be caught alone at night in the woods," excused Ronin as he tried to divert Ari's attention. Ari smirked as he finished.

"Hmm, but I reckon such a scenario would be far from unlucky. I cannot deny how much I wish it had instead been him cowering in fear beneath my feet some days ago. If it had, the demonstration of my powers would have been far more... profound," declared Ari as she dramatically clenched her fist. Ronin suspected that if such a case were to become reality, Ari would more than live up to her word. Still though, he was undecided on whether he should be feeling reassured or offended.

"As much as I'd like to see that, I'll have to be hoping for your misfortune," said Ronin as he rose from his seat. "Shall we then?" he asked while gesturing to the exit, but Ari had other plans in mind.

"I don't wish to end our little adventure on such a sour note. There's another place around here I enjoy visiting; a quaint little bridge between the hilltops that overlooks the lands for a gorgeous view."

"Are you sure that's a good idea? I thought you wanted to get back before dark?" Ronin asked while trying to conceal the stress he felt from her suggestion.

"Oh please. It's hardly past midday. We have plenty of time. Or has spending the day with me truly been so unpleasant?" she continued with a teasing whimper.

"N-no! Of course it hasn't!" Ronin answered a little too reassuringly. "Let's just be quick though. Truth be told, I'm not sure how much longer I'll be able to lug around all of these supplies for." He then slipped the rather large and heavy backpack on again. Ari giggled as she watched him stumble to the side a bit before regaining balance.

"Worry not, we won't take long," she said with a wink.

If their venture together had occurred just a few months earlier in the summer, Ronin was certain that the trek up the steep hills of Meadow's Peak would have proven fatal to him via either a sudden fit of heatstroke, himself toppling down the hill like a loose barrel, or more than likely a combination of the two. Nevertheless, he slowly trudged his way up the various slopes and steps until he and Ari got roughly halfway up the hill. A cozy looking bridge lay off to the side of the main road, and lead into the other half of the city below them. Ari strolled over to the midpoint of the bridge and rested her arms atop its stone railing, motioning for Ronin to join her. He moved to stand by her side and gazed out onto the scenery ahead. The large hill the city was built around stood by its lonesome in an otherwise vast sea of plains to the north and forests to the south, giving them a pristine view from the bridge. Golden crops and babbling brooks stretched far and wide in the distance, while little specks of farm animals and caravans dotted themselves all across the fields and roads.

Beyond all that lay the vibrant blue and green blur that made up the horizon. It was a beautiful, yet somewhat puzzling experience Ronin thought; to have one's sight be obstructed by nothing more than the mere limitations of the human eye. It vaguely reminded him of the walls and gates of Meadow's Peak itself, a barrier through which the world both started and ended, depending on one's point of view.

"Magnificent, is it not?" asked Ari.

"It certainly is. Perhaps I shall become a bit more of a tourist after all," said Ronin. Ari smirked softly.

"Tell me, when you first arrived here, which direction did you come from?" Ronin paused for a second to take a closer look at the many long roads that branched out from the city.

"There," he said, pointing to one of the smaller paths emerging from the east.

"Aye, and what lies beyond there?"

"Not too much I'm afraid, at least not for some distance," answered Ronin with a shrug of his shoulders. "I was on the road for about six days before arriving here. Before that though I was in Solaris, a large port city."

"Oh? And what is it like there?"

"It's a strange place honestly. It has been locked in a power struggle for some time between the church and you'll never guess who." Ronin turned to look at Ari, who raised an eyebrow as if to ask who he was referring to. "Party goers," he continued. "The expansive docks of Solaris bring in fine drink and exotic food from the shores of distant realms, so for ages the city has been infested with perhaps more black out drunkards than rats. Now that the church has just recently started to build new places of worship within the city, they're of course attempting to tone down such 'dangerous rituals.'"

"I've no doubt that such a battle will take a heavy toll on both sides," replied Ari through a series of chuckles. "People certainly desire eternal happiness after life, but seldom feel like sacrificing pleasure in the moment for it, much less anything else."

"Now that's something I can relate to," said Ronin in a matter-of-fact-like tone.

"Not very religious now are you then?"

"Orphans typically get sent to school with nuns. They taught me how to pray and attend sermons. For years as a child, I prayed for no more than some respite from the moving around and uncertainty of living. Yet my feet always remained just as blistered as ever." Ronin shook his head in annoyance.

"Hmm. You almost make me feel guilty for dragging you down the road here then. Almost," teased Ari. "I do sympathize though. Knowing what I do about the world does make it rather difficult to believe much of what the holy text has to preach, and the fact that I would without doubt be dragged to the depths of this city's dungeon and relentlessly tormented to death were my identity to be discovered definitely doesn't encourage me to have much faith either."

Ronin paused to think to himself. Hearing Ari's words frightened him. He knew that attempting to practice witchcraft, real or not, was forbidden by the church, but he never realized that the punishment would be quite that severe. He then shuddered as he considered that he too was technically wanted for heresy by the church now. If they were to find out the truth, there would be no trial nor sanctuary for him. Ronin turned to Ari, wanting to express his concern, but stopped as Ari let out a loud gasp and looked away from him. Ronin followed her gaze, and a short distance ahead, saw a small, filthy looking boy staring at Ari in fear as he clutched her coin purse tightly in his hand, before spinning around and sprinting away. As he fled, Ari growled with enough anger to make even Ronin flinch briefly, before she absentmindedly ran off after the little thief.

Ronin also gave chase, and quickly overtook Ari despite the added weight he was carrying. He dashed around the exit corner of the bridge, and saw the boy running down the steep road back towards the market. The boy nimbly spun around and vaulted over whatever obstacles came his way be them bewildered passersby or loose boxes, and Ronin followed suit. He ran so fast down the hill that his cloak was left soaring after him. As infuriating as this situation certainly was for Ari, Ronin still had to fight back a smile as he took pleasure in being the chaser rather than the runner for once. The boy's botched attempt at a stealthy pickpocket combined with his obviously far more experienced running ability was a dead giveaway that he was new to being a thief, and had seen his fair share of failure thus far. Having been in this boy's shoes just a few years ago, Ronin could easily guess what kind of terrifying thoughts were bouncing around in his head. Being captured and turned over to the guards would ordinarily mean a hefty fine (that the boy certainly couldn't afford) at best, and a severed hand at worst, and that was assuming that the person who did the capturing wasn't interested in inflicting some even harsher punishment themselves. Though Ronin felt more sympathetic than most folk probably would.

Despite the boy's practiced maneuvers, he was still outmatched even by virtue of Ronin's longer legs alone. The boy looked over his shoulder as he neared the base of the hill, and his eyes went wide as he saw how close Ronin was to catching him. Without a second of hesitation, the boy dashed to his left, vaulted over the side of the road, and dropped into the congested back alleys of the city beside it. Ronin quickly arrived at the boy's drop point, but stopped dead in his tracks as he watched him disappear into the maze of slums ahead; the very same maze Ronin had been nearly captured in just a few days ago. Ronin's heart was pounding, and his legs itched to continue his pursuit, but he knew it would be risky. Finding the boy would be far more difficult now that he had a near limitless amount of potential hiding spots. There was also the possibility that he could be running to regroup with a whole gang of delinquents, at which point Ronin and Ari would likely be cornered and stripped of far more than their pocket change. Ronin continued to weigh the risk in his head, but stopped when he heard a mild crashing sound. He looked in the direction it had come from, and saw that Ari had dropped down into the alleys herself, and soon vanished in between the many buildings as well.

"Ari wait!" Ronin called out to no response. He knew he needed to follow her; the risk of a wealthy and attractive looking girl like Ari getting harassed or lost in the slums was high. He jumped down into the crevices, and was surprised by how much his new and sturdy boots eased the landing. As Ronin ran into the winding paths in search of Ari, the entire area quickly turned gloomy and foreboding in his mind. Ronin no longer felt at home inside of these shaded, isolated alleyways.

Ronin called Ari's name repeatedly as he dashed and ducked around every corner and building in sight.

"Over here!" he eventually heard her call back from somewhere nearby. Ronin started running in the direction of her voice, but doubled his pace when he suddenly heard Ari shriek. He spun around the next corner so fast that he nearly tripped over his own momentum. When Ronin steadied himself, he looked up to see Ari, groaning and collapsed in a pile of shattered crates and debris. Ronin stepped over to take her hand and help lift Ari to her feet.

"Are you alright?" he asked worrisomely.

"I'm f-fine..." Ari's voice was quiet and sounded equally despaired and angry. She shook in place slightly, clearly in pain, and looked down to see that her clothes were littered with dirt and small tears. Ari frustratedly did her best to brush herself off, to little effect.

"Who did this to you?"

"No one... I fell," said Ari, who sounded fully embarrassed.

"Oh..." Ronin was surprised but at least relieved she hadn't been attacked. "Look, we should just go back to the coven now. This place isn't safe, especially after dark,"

"We can't just let that thief escape!" snapped Ari.

"Why not?! He only got away with a few coins, and judging from what we're wearing you must have plenty more money buried away somewhere."

"I don't care about the money!"

"Then why are we here?! That kid is long gone by now. The second we lost sight of him he might as well have vanished to a different world. Is this just because of your pride?"

"Do not speak to me of pride!" screamed Ari. Ronin felt greatly taken aback as her anger was swiftly redirected at him personally.

They looked away from each other after that, and neither one of them said another word at first. Ronin started to rest his aching body, and watched out of the corner of his eye as Ari leaned against a wall to do the same.

"I'm sorry... " she said softly. "That was unnecessary of me. I am just... ashamed of the truth."

Ronin sighed softly and moved closer to her.

"One of the things I've learned about being a complete nobody, is that you're never really in much of a position to be judging others all that harshly," he said. Ari smirked weakly.

"That coin purse the boy stole, Jey made it for me when we were kids. He told me that wandering the world isn't cheap, so when I finally get my chance to do just that, I'd need an easy way to store my funds." Ari's voice began to crack as she continued. "I know this will sound foolish, but without the purse that whole dream just doesn't feel as right anymore." Ari frowned, and slid down the wall to take a seat as she finished talking. Ronin turned to do the same. For once, he genuinely felt like he understood where Ari was coming from.

"Sentimentality feels strongest when we think we have nothing else to hold on to. Maybe that feeling of yours is true, or maybe it isn't. Either way, losing the purse means you'll finally get to find out for certain," Ronin said nervously. "Fate has a cruel sense of humor for bringing us opposites together. Perhaps we should try switching lives for some time."

"I wish, but I'm afraid there are no spells for that," said Ari as she smiled softly at him. The two of them shared a few sorrowful laughs before standing back up. "You know... " Ari began as she reached out to place a hand on Ronin's arm. "I find it hard to believe that you are the same boy who struggled to share a drink with me just a short while ago," she said teasingly.

"Ah-" stumbled Ronin as his face went red. "You know, the atmosphere of that tavern was a little much. I'm far more accustomed to these kinds of environments." He gestured to the many filthy and broken-down buildings around them. Ari giggled at his poor excuse before they both turned to leave.

As he and Ari waded their way through the labyrinth of alleyways back towards the market, Ronin mostly relied on his instincts and familiarity with the general environment to help guide them through. Many of the paths were shaded by various tarps, rooftops, and other obstructions that shielded them from the daylight to some extent. Despite how acquainted Ronin was with such locations, he usually remained wary of any particularly dark areas just to be safe. Now however, such areas felt ironically comforting, seeing as how they could essentially be considered near limitless sources of ammunition for shadow magic wielders. Still though, he remained on guard, seeing as how calling himself a witch was still a very generous notion, and also that Ari wouldn't want to use any of her magic unless she had no other choice

The longer Ronin and Ari trudged through the claustrophobic slums, the less pleasant their surroundings became. The paths grew narrower in some parts, and more congested by filthy puddles and piles of debris and trash that the city's maintenance workers clearly couldn't be bothered to attend to so long as it was out of sight of the general public. Though she didn't say much about it, Ari's distaste for their borderline hazardous route was obvious enough.

"So... you just hang out in places like this when you have time to kill?" she asked in what seemed like the least judgmental tone she could muster.

"Sometimes. The quietness and privacy around here can be relaxing, especially after a long day of traveling."

"Fair enough, but I am sure that there must be some more, um, hygienic places that offer such pleasantries."

"What can I say?" said Ronin with a shrug. "The world isn't all party cities and wide horizons."

Ronin expected Ari to quip back at him, but all he heard instead was an irritated grunt. He looked back over his shoulder and saw Ari yanking her foot out of a murky puddle she'd accidentally stepped in. He chuckled discreetly as he watched her grimace while still futilely trying to clean her even further stained clothes.

"Hurry up. These alleys aren't usually very safe, especially for princesses." Ari's face snapped towards him with a scowl as she heard his taunt. She marched over and stood before him with her arms crossed.

"If it's danger you're so concerned about, then I fear for your safety far more than my own. Or have you so quickly forgotten which one of us rescued the other after a near lethal mugging?"

"Ah... point taken." Ronin uncomfortably rubbed his neck and tried to avoid her threatening gaze. "At least stay close to me, just in case."

"You sure are acting rather chivalrous all of sudden. It's awfully sweet, but wholly unnecessary." Ari emphasized her point by reaching down to pick up a small rock off the ground. She then entangled it in a sphere of shadows, before clenching her fist tightly. Ronin couldn't see what was happening to the rock, but he soon heard a harsh grinding or crunching sound, and when Ari released the shadows, all that was left in her grasp was a handful of sand and dust that trickled its way down to the ground. Ronin visibly shook in place as he watched, making Ari chuckle.

As they continued on their way, Ronin grew puzzled by the layout of the paths. Many of the branching alleys around them were blocked off by large piles of ruin and debris. Ordinarily, such a sight in and of itself wasn't anything remarkable, given how abundant all the discarded trash was. It was the sheer number of obstructed routes, the likes of which forced him and Ari down a single, winding path, that Ronin found odd. Eventually, they came upon an empty, stretched out path between two long and tall buildings, with the only exit in sight being at the far end of the path.

Ronin paused just outside the entrance, an instinctive shiver of his skin telling him that something wasn't right. Ari didn't seem to notice his hesitation though, and continued walking in the only direction that was available to them. She made it several steps forward before Ronin lunged forward and grabbed her by the wrist. Ari shook at his sudden grasp.

"What is it?" she asked anxiously.

"Something's not right..." whispered Ronin as he surveyed the rooftops. "We're going back. Now," he declared strictly, before yanking Ari back towards the way they had entered from.

"But wait what's happening-" began Ari before gasping as she and Ronin looked ahead to witness a menacing figure brandishing a shiny short sword leap down from his hiding spot on the buildings above, cutting off their escape. The assailant was wearing a dark green cloak that Ronin recognized immediately. He shook for a fraction of a second as he realized what was going on, before turning around and dashing across the alley way to the far exit, still dragging Ari along closely. They made it about halfway down the path before a second figure emerged from around a corner to block them. With one of his gloved hands, he wielded a slim, serrated dagger, while the other clutched a hand-crossbow, its fine steel bolt aimed directly at Ronin, and dripping ever so slightly with what had to be some kind of poison coating.

Ronin and Ari's feet froze in place as they desperately searched for any way to escape as their ambushers slowly closed in on them.

"We have no trouble with you," called out Ronin. "Take whatever you like then we'll be on our way." Ronin knew that reasoning with these two was probably pointless, but he figured his odds would be better than if he tried to intimidate them, seeing as how they were currently dancing their blades in their hands and snickering all the while as if deriving some sadistic pleasure from their actions.

"Stay close to me... " Ronin heard Ari whisper as they stood back to back. He took a deep breath, and braced himself for whatever Ari was planning to do. However, nothing happened in the seconds that followed, and all Ronin heard was a sly, familiar laughter coming from the rooftops above.

"Aha! Alright Emil, I'll admit it; you've more than proven your worth." Ronin and Ari looked up to see Zane, who stared down at them with his legs swaying over the ledge like a child, and his face contorted into a snarky grin to match. And sitting beside him, was the same boy who had stolen Ari's coin purse, though instead of his former rags, he now wore a smaller version of the Darkwood hunter uniform.

"You were right master. They are beyond gullible," said the boy as Zane patted his back before leaping down in front of Ronin and Ari.

"I suppose you now find yourself wishing you'd heeded my advice," he said to Ronin while nodding his head towards Ari. "Stubborn to the end, isn't she?"

"Z-Zane?!" stumbled Ari before anyone else could get a word in. She looked at him with an expression of worry that quickly shifted into one of rage as the absurdity of the situation dawned on her. "Is this some cruel joke?! Have you honestly gone through the effort of trapping us here just because I rejected you?" Zane scoffed at her accusation.

"My oh my, my dearest Ariana. I will admit that I've been disappointed by your many rejections, and that witnessing you spend your time with this meager companion of yours was not particularly enjoyable. Ironically though, I must also confess that I'm feeling rather prideful that you claim to think so little of me now."

"It's hardly a thought I've recently developed," snapped Ari, who was rapidly growing more enraged by Zane's arrogance. "Explain yourself. What reason have you to ambush us like this?"

"If you would cease your incessant self-flattery for but one short moment, you'd surely answer your own question!" Zane shouted at her, his anger once again manifesting in an instant. "You're not the one who matters anymore," he declared while lowering his hood to give Ronin a challenging stare. He extended his arm for a handshake. "Now then, how about that name of yours? Seeing as how we clearly have business together now." Ronin remained silent. Like Ari, he too was furious, and chided himself for falling for Zane's ruse. Unlike Ari though, he was currently about as defenseless as a cornered rat. He thought carefully about what to do and say, but before he could make any decisions, his hesitation was swiftly punished as Zane formed a fist with the hand he'd offered and gave Ronin a harsh punch to the gut. Ronin groaned loudly as he bent forward and held his

135

abdomen tightly, only to shriek in pain again as Zane swiftly shot his knee upwards, colliding it with Ronin's chin and causing him to fly back and slam against the wall behind him. His backpack absorbed part of the impact as the sound of the glass potion bottles shattering ringed throughout the alley.

Ari gasped worriedly, and knelt down to help Ronin.

"Zane you fiend!" she screamed as she wiped away the streaks of blood that oozed out of Ronin's nose and mouth. Ronin tried to compose himself, he could feel Ari clinging to his shirt tightly, her hands trembling as if she were a bomb about to explode in fury.

"I've asked nicely twice, I won't do so a third time," said Zane angrily as he stood over Ronin and skillfully drew a sharp throwing knife from within his sleeve. "Tell me your name," he demanded.

"Ronin!" shouted Ari before Ronin had a chance to even think. "His name is Ronin... "

"Ronin," said Zane with a satisfied smirk. "You have no idea how glad I am to finally meet you." Ronin shivered at Zane's words. For reasons a nobody like himself couldn't begin to imagine, Zane and his Darkwood Hunters wanted him, and no one else.

Zane crouched down in front of Ronin and Ari with no resistance from either of them. He stared at Ronin for a second, but then reached out towards a small puddle that had formed from the dripping coming from Ronin's backpack. He ran his fingers through the strange dark liquid before raising them to his nose for a sniff.

"Hm, a concentration potion among others if I'm not mistaken. A rather odd under the table purchase for a couple of seemingly ordinary youths." Zane reached a hand forward and tugged lightly at Ronin's fine clothes, smearing the potion substance against them in the process. "You know back in the tavern, I honestly wasn't sure if you were the person we've been looking for, what with this fancy get up of yours and all. Of course, none of this would've been a problem if old William hadn't gone after you on his own. I guess the entirety of the reward sounded too enticing. Just to be safe though, why don't you give me your best confession?"

"W-what are you talking about...?" stuttered Ronin through a few bloodied coughs.

"Heh... you really have no idea what you've gotten yourself into. Don't you?" Ronin said nothing back.

"Allow me to paint you a picture then," began Zane with a smirk. "This past summer, the days went by much as they usually do for most folk, myself included. Crops were tended, sales bartered, bounties collected, you get the idea," he patronized. "But then one day, something unusual happens, something no one, not even I expected. A hushed voice utters a whisper, and from it is born a rumor that is carried by the wind to every nook and cranny buried across the realm. A rumor claiming that a young, mysterious, and particularly stupid boy is wandering around Rendolyn in possession of a certain item that

137

he yearns to learn more about. He asks priests, chroniclers, essentially anyone educated enough to read. Unfortunately for him though, no one seems to be able to help, and so he continues to travel from town to town, forming the most linear, predictable pattern one can imagine. Does any of this sound familiar to you, Ronin?" It was nigh impossible for Ronin to keep his nerve. He could feel his bones trembling beneath his skin, but still fought hard to not relent to Zane's attempts to draw information from him.

"No..." Ronin lied near hopelessly.

"I see..." replied Zane. He glared at Ronin some more, only this time his face lacked any of its previous guile or mockery, and instead looked to be filled purely with focus and determination. "So, this means nothing to you then?" Zane asked as he reached into his pocket and withdrew the small crest adorned handcloth that Ronin had lost. Zane gently unfolded it in his hands, taking one long look at the decorative raven sewn into the fabric before holding it open right in front of Ronin's still bloodied face. At last, Ronin's eyes betrayed him, and he found himself at a loss for words as he looked ahead with shock. The handcloth that he had carried with him for years, for his entire life as a matter of fact now looked... different.

The crest and fabric themselves were still the same, but now something else sat alongside them. Strange markings, or perhaps characters from a language Ronin didn't recognize were now inscribed onto the fabric beside the raven, which stared straight at them. The symbols weren't ordinarily sewn into the material though, rather they looked to be sort of floating just ever so slightly above the knots, and they possessed a bizarre, almost transparent blue glow that highlighted them from everything else. Ronin was utterly baffled, and continued to stare at the symbols wordlessly. Zane saw his reaction and pounced on it immediately by quickly drawing another knife from his sleeve and holding it to Ronin's throat.

"Answer me now Ronin! I'm no longer in the mood for games. Is this yours?" Zane demanded to know while nearly shoving the handcloth in Ronin's face.

"Okay, okay!" shouted Ronin as he snapped out of his trance. His head throbbed tremendously, and he could feel his heart pounding faster and faster with each passing second. "Yes, it's my cloth, but I know nothing of it I swear!"

"Then how did you get it?" pressed Zane.

"I-It's just some random piece of childhood memorabilia! I've had it for as long as I can remember. It has no value, it's purely sentimental!" Zane looked at Ronin skeptically. His imposing aura felt as sharp as his daggers, but he eventually stood back up. He brushed some dirt off his pants and chuckled softly to himself, seeming to have partially reverted back to his more easygoing persona.

"You aren't lying. I can see it in your eyes," he said confidently. Ronin looked up at Zane.

"The crest, what is it?" Ronin was panting still, feeling desperate, but also undeniably curious. Zane did little more than shrug in reply.

"I'm afraid I can't really tell you anything about it my friend. I myself had never seen it until around a month or so ago."

"Then what is this all about?!"

"I hate to break this to you Ronin, but after hearing about your recent escapades, it appears that someone has decided to put a pretty sizable bounty out for your capture." Ronin felt himself go faint as Zane confirmed his most dreaded suspicions. Witches, magic, ambushes, and now an enormous bounty on his head? It all felt so surreal, like a dream he craved to awaken from. He spat out flurries of fragmented words, his mind trying to ask a dozen questions all at once but managing to speak no more than garbled gibberish.

"Whoa, slow down there. If it's any consolation, I'd probably feel equally distressed if I were in your position," said Zane. "It's rather strange, you know? We were all ecstatic when we found your cloth by William's body; a fortune larger than we could conceive, weaved into such a small and delicate thing. But it's owner? Nowhere to be found. We searched the whole of those woods until we found the cave you presumably fell into, but by then, you were no more than a trail of footprints leading into the woods... a trail that mysteriously vanished after some time." Zane briefly glared at Ari. "But then, as if through some stroke of divine fortune, a few days go by, and look who comes wandering into town? A strange individual whose face looks to match most of our descriptions, and one who is accompanied by Ariana here nonetheless, a bizarre lass herself who frequently comes and goes through those very same woods, as I am well aware." Ari cringed as Zane all but admitted to stalking her. "It was a gamble picking on you, I will admit, but it seems my patience has at last been rewarded in plenty," declared Zane proudly.

Zane then turned to his followers.

"Emil!" he shouted to the boy on the rooftops. "Go fetch our nearest patrol group, then tell everyone else to prepare the horses. We've got a long journey ahead of us." The boy grunted in affirmation, then swiftly dashed away as Zane turned to the sword wielding hunter beside him. "Bind his hands. I want him escorted out of the city as quickly and discreetly as possible." Finally, he looked to his third hunter. "We can't afford any distractions. Kill the girl."

Ronin panicked as the man took his crossbow and aimed it straight at Ari's face. Time seemed to freeze for him; he could barely hear Ari's gasps or the shifting of the man's weapon in his arms. Ronin was instantly devoured by guilt as he realized that his own ignorance was about to get Ari, the girl who had shown him unwavering kindness, heartlessly executed. The man moved his finger to the crossbow's trigger, and any instincts of self-preservation Ronin had vanished. He wanted to run at him, but before he could even move a muscle he was forced to reel back as the air around them all suddenly exploded into a cloud of darkness.

The effect was near instantaneous. One moment, everything around Ronin looked plain as day, and the next, he, Zane, and everyone else were consumed by a blackened shroud. Ronin shielded his eyes instinctively, but opened them again shortly after. The power of his shadow magic granted him sight of what was happening. A wide storm of howling shadows and darkness was swirling around them at speeds faster than he could comprehend, creating a growing vortex that seemed to be swallowing Zane and his hunters whole. And in the center of it all, he saw Ari. She stood strong, her open palms pressed together tightly, almost as if she were offering a prayer, and through the wailing cry of the spell, he could discern her own screams of fury as she unleashed the might and aggression she had built up against their foes.

A moment later, the shadowy vortex dissipated, and a grim silence encompassed the two of them, save for the abrupt yet brief noises of Zane and his troops collapsing to the ground. Ronin slowly rose to his feet, and looked over at Ari with his jaw wide.

"Is... is it over?" he asked through heavy pants. Ari nodded at him slowly. Ronin glanced down at their fallen attackers. The spell appeared to have left them significantly bruised and bludgeoned, but Ronin noticed that they were in fact still breathing.

"When they wake, won't they know about you?"

"When they wake? What?!" Ari then to looked to see for herself that Zane and his hunters had survived her spell. "That's impossible..." she said weakly before stumbling over and collapsing into a wall.

"Ari!" Ronin shouted as he stepped over to her. He helped Ari balance herself, then brushed her hair aside from her face. Ari's eyes slowly blinked open and shut, as if she were struggling to stay awake. "What's wrong?!"

"I-I don't know..." she mumbled.

Ronin stared at her with concern. His ears were then filled with the sounds of trampling footsteps coming from the direction of the far exit, and they were quickly closing in on their position.

"We have to get out of here!" Ari grunted in agreement, then shook her head to try and snap herself out of her sudden and bizarre fatigue. Ari started running towards the other exit, and Ronin moved to follow her, but paused briefly as something caught his eye. Resting on the ground beside Zane, was his handcloth, the mysterious characters still glowing ominously besides the crest. He swiftly reached down and grabbed the cloth before stuffing it into his pocket and chasing after Ari.

They made haste back into the cluster of alleys, until they found themselves in a clearing between the buildings, from which many other paths branched out from. Ari froze and stared at the many routes they could take, until Ronin snatched her by the wrist and started sprinting off towards another alley to their right. They could still hear the shouts and footsteps of their newfound pursuers echoing nearby. Ronin knew that they were for all intents and purposes trapped in a maze with these thugs, but the labyrinthine terrain that attempted to seal their demise was also one of their strongest assets for survival. It may have been extending the chase, but it also made them immensely more difficult to find. Eventually, Ronin dashed around a corner and saw a tall wooden fence blocking their path. He peeked in between the boards and saw the marketplace straight ahead. He breathed a sigh of relief and ran forward in an effort to scale the fence, but stopped in his tracks as he felt his hand get pulled back by a feeble grasp.

"Ronin, something isn't right... I feel... I..." Ari's breathing was slow and heavy, and her eyes flickered open and shut again and again while her legs stood shakily. She looked ready to pass out at any second.

"Just a little further Ari! Please!" Ronin dashed over and lifted her arm behind his neck to help carry her.

"I... I can't..."

Ronin could hear the noises behind them getting louder, he knew they only had mere moments left before they were caught.

"Hide... hide we have to hide!" Ronin searched around until he noticed a small nook in between a few walls off to their side. He gently carried Ari over to it and rested her down before placing a few loose crates and sacks in front of them to help block the view. The men giving search for them were mere seconds away now, and Ronin shook anxiously in place, fully aware that there was nowhere to run anymore, and that if those men were to take even a somewhat close look in their direction, their location would almost surely be discovered. He repeatedly shot his eyes back and forth between the pathway ahead and Ari to his side. Her eyes were shut, and Ronin wondered if she'd fainted, until he saw her weakly make the slightest of motions with one hand. In the next moment, a thin veil of darkness filled the crevices of their hiding spot, blocking out the already shaded daylight. Ronin thought that such a sight would look quite bizarre to any ordinary person, but could only hope that it would be discreet enough that no one would notice from a distance.

He looked ahead and saw at least a half a dozen uniformed hunters run into the alleyway in front of them. They glanced around in circles, searching their surroundings. Ronin could feel Ari shaking beside him. Her eyes remained shut tight, and her teeth were grit hard. The exertion of maintaining the spell was clearly tearing away at what little remained of her strength. As one of the thugs turned to look right in their direction, Ronin quickly reached his hand forward to cover Ari's mouth and silence her progressively louder breathing. After another moment, the men shrugged frustratedly and ran off. As soon as they were gone, Ronin whispered for Ari to lower the spell. Her arm collapsed to her side, and her head toppled over onto Ronin's shoulder. The two of them rested in place for a brief moment before Ronin got up, lifted Ari's arm behind his neck again and all but dragged her forward.

"You did it Ari, you saved us," he said but Ari was no longer responding.

Chapter Five
Between The Fangs

The world was dark, or at least as dark as it could look through the gaze of one born with shadow magic. Ari slowly and achingly raised her hands to her face and began to rub her eyes, groaning softly as she did so. She was lying down, and could feel a hard, lumpy surface beneath her back. After a short moment, she sat up in place and glanced around at her surroundings. The space she sat in was cylindrical almost, with jagged rocks forming walls around her. Ari felt an eerie sense of familiarity envelop her, and somehow, she recognized this place to be same the cave she'd sometimes hide in when distressed.

Ari couldn't even begin to rationalize just how she could possibly be here now. In fact, her memory as a whole felt quite hazy. She turned around to where she recalled the exit would be, but stopped in place. She looked ahead with wide eyes and shaking legs, as she came to the horrific realization that the exit was blocked off. Dozens of massive rocks lay clustered in the pathway, as if a huge cave-in had occurred. Faced with no other options, she turned back around and began to frightfully tread deeper into the empty abyss.

Ari walked for what felt like hours, with the thumping of her footsteps over stone filling her ears, and serving as her only respite from the otherwise maddening silence that seemed to infest the cavern. She felt so bitterly alone, enough so that the thought of encountering a savage cave dweller or cavern beast sounded almost appealing.

Nevertheless, she continued onwards, with the walls beside her looking so alike that she eventually started to wonder if she was actually moving at all, or if she were no more than a mouse trapped in a wheel.

After a while, the path ahead came to an end, sealed off by another solid wall of blackened stone. Ari shuddered heavily, her whole body feeling cold all of sudden as she stared at the end of her newfound prison. She wanted to scream, but barely managed to keep herself calm. Ari turned around once more, hoping that she'd missed another path somewhere along the way. She made it no more than a handful of steps forward though, before all of a sudden, a large crack appeared in the ceiling. She gasped and took a leap backwards, then witnessed something large plummet to the ground in front of her.

Once the dust had settled, Ari took a careful look, and discovered that it was a person who had fallen from the ceiling of the cavern. She shimmied over to them, and knelt down by their side only to realize that it was in fact Ronin, who lay unconscious on his back beside her. Ari felt a strange, throbbing pain overtake her as relief and horror clashed violently within her mind. She didn't know whether to be grateful that she was no longer alone, or mortified that they may be trapped here together. She felt his neck, and found a faint pulse. She then grabbed him by the shoulders and tried to gently shake him awake.

"Ronin?! Ronin, wake up!" she cried desperately, but he remained silent and motionless. Ari gave up trying to rouse him after a few minutes, and instead clung tightly to his shirt, trying her hardest to fight back the tears of fear that welled in her eyes.

But then, Ari started to feel something else. Her chest began to ache and feel tight. She perked up like a rabbit hearing the treads of a predator nearby. Her eyes opened wide before she forcefully shoved herself away from Ronin, crawling back towards the wall of the cave and practically slamming herself against it. This new sensation was quickly growing stronger. It was a power-ful craving, a bone shuddering, mind controlling, nigh insatiable feeling of hunger that spread beyond her lips and infected every fiber of her being. To any ordinary person, such a feeling was all but incomprehensible... but to Ari, it felt as familiar as an itch on her shoulder.

Ari knew her time was running out. Out of sheer panic, she quickly stripped off her travel coat and buried her face in it, childishly hoping that it would make her disappear. Her constant trembles matched the tempo of the passing seconds as they continued to tick by, each one feeling agonizingly long. She knew she needed to stay focused, to control herself. She concentrated all of her attention on the first thing that came to mind; a memory. A memory of a sound.

"*Thump... thump... thump...* " it went; the sound of Ronin's beating heart after she'd first rescued him. Such a memory now felt like a fleeting fantasy. But it wasn't, Ari told herself over and over. It was reality; the reality she'd fight to hold on to for as long as her own heart continued to beat. The pain within Ari grew worse. It felt as if thousands of hot needles were piercing their way through her flesh. She bit down on her coat as hard as she could, and listened to his heartbeat in her head over and over again. She frantically fought to make sure that it was all that existed to her, trying to tune out everything else in the world.

"Thump... thump... thump... thump... thu... th... t..."

"..."

With an awful cry, Ari tossed her coat aside. She crawled back over to the still unconscious Ronin. When she arrived, she knelt beside him, and grabbed him tightly by the face with both hands, her nails aggressively digging into his flesh like claws. She slowly inched her face ever closer to his own. A waning voice within her pleaded for her to stop, to be strong, but she swatted it aside again and again like a bug, until it faded away entirely. Her mind was emptied, and all she could feel was immense, writhing agony. And all she wanted was to make it go away. In the next second, Ari lunged down.

And then, for one of the first times in her life, Ari's world went pitch black.

A soft pitter patter was heard throughout a small and cramped room, as Ronin's fingers danced up and down atop a large barrel. With his other hand, he propped his head up by the chin and patiently watched over his companion in front of him, a torn expression spread across his face. Ari lay passed out on top of a wooden bench, with Ronin's folded up cloak serving as a pillow beneath her head. Her breathing was weak, but steady, as if she had fainted from a hard day's work under the sun.

Ashamedly, Ronin thought back to the many times he'd stolen from others in the interests of his own wellbeing. Such criminal acts often resulted in their own chases, and even some prolonged hunts on occasion, so Ronin thought that if were to have encountered their present situation by himself as per usual, then he would have already enacted some sort of plan to escape from the city and be off to wherever else the road may lead. But that was not an option for now. Presently, all he could do was wait, and hope that Ari would wake soon. Seeing her like this, especially given the dire circumstances they had been forced into, felt puzzling to him. It was a strange, unfamiliar, and somewhat helpless or guilty feeling for Ronin, to be able to do little aside from wait due to the needs of another. After all of the selfishness and wickedness he'd seen in his life, he wondered just how many people ever felt this way. A few quiet, selfish thoughts tried to continuously creep their way into Ronin's mind. He figured that even when Ari woke up, she would likely still feel rather weak. If he truly wanted to flee from Meadow's Peak, his best bet would be to do so alone. He forced such thoughts out of his head though. Staying in the city with the hunters roaming around could mean death, but as he pictured the empty country roads he'd spent so much time walking over, they hardly looked like life.

Ronin let out a soft sigh, and reached into his pocket to retrieve his hand cloth. He unfolded it and laid it out flat across the barrel. Looking at it now, it was almost as if the crest and fabric no longer existed to him; all he could give any attention to were those bizarre symbols. He glanced back and forth between Ari and the cloth, and knew that right now he needed her perhaps more than she needed him. The sudden appearance of these symbols gave Ronin a lingering suspicion that she and the other witches would probably be his only chance at finally finding some answers for why Zane was after him. Or for who Zane was after so to speak...

He slipped deeper into focus, his mind racing with possibilities, until he nearly jumped from his seat as Ari out of nowhere shot up to a sitting position, letting out a loud yelp as she did so. She had her back turned to Ronin and was panting heavily, though she said nothing and made no motion to turn around.

"Ari..." Ronin called out to her, but she said nothing back to him. He called her name a few more times before reaching over to shake her by the shoulder. As soon as he touched her, Ari shrieked and spun around to see him. They stared at each other, quiet and motionless, with Ronin's face being one of worry and bewilderment, and Ari's one of panic and shock.

"Ari? It's me. It's Ronin," Ronin said as he slowly stepped over to her.

"Ronin..." Ari mumbled. She fought to breathe as sweat streaked down her forehead. Ronin sat beside her on the bench.

"Are you okay?"

"I... I don't know." Ari was still shaking, and could hardly even look at Ronin as she spoke. "Where are we?" she asked as she finally took a look around.

"A backroom in Bertram's store. It was the closest place I could think to bring you where we could maybe get help. You were unconscious for about an hour."

"Only an hour..." muttered Ari while rubbing her face.

"Does this happen often? I guess you weren't joking when you said that spells require energy."

"It was simply a very powerful spell is all," answered Ari quickly and dismissively. "Still though... it shouldn't have been that draining."

A loud knocking sound was then heard at a door behind them, and it soon swung open as Bertram stepped inside carrying a large mug of water in one hand.

"I thought I heard some voices in here. Didn't I tell you to pace yourself at the tavern, lassie? Ronin here said he had to lug you across the entire market!" Bertram laughed as he handed Ari the mug and patted her on the back.

"Oh um, right... I'll remember that next time," stumbled Ari confusedly before taking a large gulp of water. Fortunately, her dazed and disoriented state did a reasonable job of passing for drunkenness.

"I'm sure you will," said Bertram sarcastically. "Rest here for a while. I'll be closing up the shop in a few hours though once the sun starts to set." On that note, Bertram bid them farewell and returned to his store.

"You didn't tell him...?" questioned Ari as she slowly turned to look at Ronin. He shrugged.

"I would hardly know what to say. I'm still trying to make sense of everything that happened myself." Ari groaned slightly, and took another sip of water. She closed her eyes and raised her hands to massage her face, and such an act seemed to jog her awareness.

"R-Ronin!" she shouted while shooting up to her feet. "We must get help at once. I won't be able to fight Zane and his hunters if they find us again!"

"I know!" said Ronin as he too stood up. "It's okay though, I do believe we will be safe here for now."

"Safe?!" Ari looked at Ronin like he was a maniac. "A roving band of bounty hunters is out for our heads, and you would think us to be safe? They're out there searching for us as we speak!"

"Calm down. I don't say this without reason." Ari took a deep breath, but continued to look at him with threatening skepticism. "Think about it. Why would Zane go through all the trouble of luring us into those isolated alleys? He and his hunters are rash and vicious, but not stupid. They won't risk engaging us in public, not when doing so could draw the attention of the city guard or even other bounty hunters who are after me for all we know."

"I see... well then what are we waiting for then? Let us go to the guards and enlighten them as to the fact that Zane and his Darkwood Hunters are but a merry band of murderous lunatics!" Ari then started to stampede towards the door.

"Wait! Slow down for a moment," replied Ronin as he moved to block her, feeling kind of like he was trying to get in the way of a charging war beast. "I hate to tell you this, but I doubt the guards here will be of much help. Zane ambushed us in the slums, and the truth is that the law in cities like Meadow's Peak is not concerned about the petty scandals that occur outside of the eye of the general public. You may masquerade as someone of class, but your pockets are just as empty as mine are right now. We aren't important to anyone, and no one saw the crime happen, therefore the guards don't care." Ronin shook his head in frustration as he finished speaking. There was a time when the reality of their circumstances, as well as his status in society, had sincerely troubled him. These days though, both were no more than common nuisances that he would gladly wave off if their lives weren't presently threatened. Ari remained silent at first, the mood of the room becoming noticeably heavier.

"I spend far too much time locked up at home, so I suppose I am rather naive to some of the harsher truths of society," said a visibly sad Ari in a soft and timid voice. "This all makes no sense though, why are they after us, nay, after you Ronin?" As she questioned him, Ari looked at Ronin with a kind of doubtful expression he hadn't seen in her eyes before. As her worrisome, perhaps even distrustful gaze pierced through his heart like a knife, Ronin felt sincerely hurt by it. It was a look that begged to ask if she truly knew him even in the slightest sense. Ronin frowned, feeling more stressed and confused now than any other time in his hollow life that came to memory. He looked back over to his side at the handcloth that was still spread out over the barrel. He reached one hand over to it, but paused right before picking it up. He wanted Ari to trust him again, but in the moment, something about showing the cloth to her in particular made him feel uneasy. He'd of course shown it and the crest to countless other people over the span of the last few months, and recalled just how many times he'd been left staring at the cloth all by his lonesome after whomever he'd sought out seemingly inevitably had no information for him.

To any ordinary person, such a repeated experience would likely be maddening, but Ronin presently realized that despite how admittedly curious he got at times, his lack of progress in his goals never actually bothered him quite as much as it probably should have. After a while, his mission felt far more about the lengthy journeys between destinations than anything else. Learning about the cloth, his family, and ultimately himself was, at least in some sense, just something to do. All of these thoughts ran through Ronin's mind as his fingers inched ever closer to the cloth. If Ari somehow really did have even the slightest hint as to what the crest and symbols meant, then she would potentially know more of his own origins than even he did.

"But would any of that really be me?" Ronin wondered. His mind was then filled with images of the coven. As recent, limited, and even plain as most of the memories were, they made a conflicting part of him wish to not know the truth.

"What do you have there?" asked Ari out of the blue. She had moved closer to Ronin on the bench and was just now beginning to look over the barrel.

"Wha-?!" gasped Ronin as he swiftly grabbed the cloth and dashed away from her. "I thought you were the sociable one, don't you know it's rude to pry into people's business like that?!" he snapped out of deflection.

"I do," said Ari as she crossed her arms. "And you'll have my apologies in due time, but for the foreseeable future we're stuck together with our lives at stake. I'm afraid your business is mine as well now." Ronin frowned slightly, Ari's words hitting hard. "We all have things we do not wish to speak of..." said Ari empathetically. "But we need to work together now." Ronin looked at Ari briefly, his chest pounding with anxiety, before he groaned out of frustration and tossed the cloth to her. In some way or another, he felt as if he was saying goodbye to someone.

"It's just a simple handcloth. It contains a crest that I believe belongs to my blood family, though I know nothing more than that, not even a name to go with it. I lost it when I was attacked the day you found me in the cave, but when Zane showed it to me earlier it had these... well just see for yourself." Ari looked at Ronin with a puzzled expression before turning her gaze down to the cloth she held between both hands. Almost immediately, her face was filled with surprise as she recognized what he'd been referring to. "Wha-what is it?!" asked Ronin impatiently.

"These symbols... " began Ari as she caressed her fingers over the almost incorporeal text. "You say you've never seen them before today?" She looked back to Ronin.

"I swear I haven't... Do you know what they are?" Ronin began to fidget uncomfortably in his seat.

"Aye. The language is Vidican, written with arcane runes; a form of spell-based writing visible only to those born into a school of magic."

"So Zane didn't see them then. What do they say?" badgered Ronin. Ari looked at the cloth again, carefully examining the raven crest and writing once more. She then turned back to Ronin and stared him in the eye with an almost intimidating strictness.

"This crest, you are positive that it belongs to your family, are you not?"

"It's the oldest item I own; I was told by orphanage caretakers as a child that it was in my possession when they found me. I can think of no other explanation."

"Very well... " began Ari. "Sil, it reads. Sil. I take it this must be your family name."

As she revealed the name to him, Ronin fell silent. He shook his head for a moment, and then scoffed quietly.

"Ronin Sil..." he said to himself. Ronin always imagined that finally learning his family name would be satisfying, at least in the sense that he'd at last have something more specific to vent his frustrations towards instead of the faceless apparitions he pictured his parents as. But hearing the name now just made it sound so empty, as if he were learning the name of some random stranger he'd never met before.

"I don't suppose the name rings any bells, does it?" asked Ari.

"On the contrary, I was hoping you could tell me about it," answered Ronin regretfully.

"Well, I'm afraid that both the name and the crest are unfamiliar to me."

"Trust me, you're far from the only one... or so I thought," said Ronin as he recalled Zane's story about the rumors surrounding Ronin's journey.

"The presence of these runes does however all but guarantee that you come from a family of witches. Ronin's head started spinning as he struggled to rationalize what Ari was telling him.

No matter what decisions he made or conclusions he came to, Ronin felt as if fate was constantly tugging his arms in different directions, to the point where he was very nearly torn in two. A strong part of him wanted nothing more than a chance to start over, to flee from his lonely and aimless life on the road, and immerse himself in a new world of magic and adventure alongside those whose hands he had fallen into so recently. The more he pursued such a desire though, the faster he thought it seemed that the painful origins he was running from managed to catch up to him, yet only ever in a way that made this alternate path of self-discovery all the more difficult to follow. Both sides of Ronin's two-faced life were inexplicably woven together in knots that perhaps no power on this earth could hope to truly unravel, and Ronin imagined himself like a capsized boat being hammered against waves and rocky shores for a lifetime.

"Splendid then!" snapped Ronin. "We have a name but are still no closer to understanding why someone out there wants me stomped out of existence like some worthless spider."

"Whoever placed the bounty clearly knows some things about you that we don't," replied Ari. "Still though,

I doubt we'll learn more through further discussion. We need to focus on getting home for now."

"You're right..." said Ronin before pausing. His head was throbbing now, and he could hardly think straight. The more he tried to consider the implications of what Ari was telling him, the more he felt as if his brain and personality were being sliced into pieces like bread. "None of this will matter anyways if we can't escape this city. And it's not like we can just walk right out the front gate and sprinkle a breadcrumb trail all the back to the coven for Zane."

"True enough..." began Ari with a slight shiver. "You seem far more, uh, accustomed... to our circumstances. What do you suggest we do?" Ronin sat up straight in his seat, and closed his eyes while holding a hand to his face tightly in contemplation. Despite his past experiences in at least somewhat similar situations, he still found himself feeling as worried and ill prepared as he could ever imagine. A wolf would spend its entire life training to hunt, whereas a rabbit would spend its own training to flee, but this certainly didn't mean they were evenly matched.

"It's not easy to say. You saw how Zane reacted when he found out who I was. If he has awakened by now, then it's only a matter of time before he figures out a way to capture us within the city... or capture me rather."

"Then we need to run. Now!" interjected Ari, who scowled in disgust at her own idea. "Maybe we could sneak out through one of the smaller gates?"

"I wish it were that easy. The open fields around Meadow's Peak provide no cover, running through them alone without some crowd to blend in to would be suicide. Also, there's no doubt that Zane also recognizes our inability to rely on the law. He will expect us to make a run for it, and he already mentioned that he has hunter patrols in and around the city." Ronin paused momentarily as he looked at Ari straight in the eye, a hopeful yet concerned expression on his face. "They can't possibly number more than two or three men per group. Do you think you can take them?" A look of offense spread over Ari's face, and her jaw dropped as if to retort such a question, but she uttered no words and frowned instead.

"We're trapped then. And what an ironic prison this is," Ari whispered sorrowfully while taking a look at the door leading into Bertram's store and by extension the rest of Meadow's Peak, then the world.

Ronin watched her with sympathy. He still didn't really believe that there was all that much worth seeing past that door, but he wasn't so inconsiderate as to tell her this in the moment.

"It's all still out there you know," he said while nodding to the door. "And I don't see any reason for the best of both worlds to also include the lesser parts of either." Ari laughed faintly at his remark.

"I'd be more inclined to believe you if the worst of both worlds weren't right outside as we speak," she said; Ronin shrugged. He found all of Ari's emotions so contagious. Whenever she frowned or pouted, he did the same. And whenever she laughed and smiled, he immediately wished he could do the same in earnest.

"My point is that we still have a chance," Ronin declared. "Zane knows we need to run, but that doesn't mean we can't outsmart him."

"Aye, though as much as I hate to admit it, he is certainly far more clever than I ever would've anticipated. I do hope you have a plan."

"I'm working on it." Ronin searched his mind for every memory he could recollect of all the dangers he had gotten himself into over the years. He scanned through every alley mugging, guard chase, and roadside robbery he'd somehow managed to live through as if they were now part of an encyclopedia of survival strategies, but could come up with no ideas. Ronin looked down and held his face in frustration. As he sat there groaning, the light shining into the room through the windows quickly dimmed, as if a cloud had passed in front of the sun.

"Wait!" exclaimed Ronin as he looked up to Ari again. Her face still looked just as clear and distinct as always. "We're being too hasty. If we make a run for it now, Zane will surely catch us. But if we can just buy time until nightfall, we'll be able to sneak out when he can't see us, but we can see everything!"

"That... might just work. We are shadow witches after all," said Ari proudly. Ronin smiled at her.

"That we are," he said before returning to his seat and propping his legs up comfortably on a crate.

"What are you doing?" asked Ari confusedly.

"Resting, as you should be. We still have a few hours to kill before sunset and Bertram already gave us permission to wait here until he closes shop."

"Oh..." replied Ari with a low sigh. Ronin closed his eyes and dipped his head backwards. The rickety wooden chair he sat in was certainly no luxurious bed, but Ronin would've settled for sleeping atop a board of nails after the day they'd been through. An astonishing three minutes went by before Ronin suddenly felt himself being shaken back to attention.

"What is it?" he asked annoyedly while pushing Ari's hands away from him.

"I cannot just sit here helplessly until after dark," she said with a tone that didn't sound willing to negotiate. Ronin silently pleaded that Ari's stubbornness wasn't about to make her suggest something reckless.

"Zane doesn't know we're here now, so it's safest to stay put. There's no reason for us to take any risks." Ari pouted at his words.

"But there's still so much we don't know. Would our position not be stronger if we had more answers?" Ronin skeptically raised an eyebrow at her question.

"What are you implying? You already said we won't learn anything more by talking."

"Not if it's just the two of us, but there is one other in Meadow's Peak who might know something about your family and the bounty. We are far from the first witches Sorem and her family have dealt with over generations. It's possible she might be able to help."

"That... might actually be worth it." Ronin scowled as he found himself tempted by Ari's idea. "Alright fine you win. But if she knows nothing, I'm leaving you behind." "Oh please," smirked Ari. "How could you do that when you're still in my debt. You may have carried me here to safety, but I have rescued you twice thus far." Ronin rolled his eyes as Ari chuckled. She then impatiently moved towards the door.

"Wait!" Ronin said as he grabbed her shoulder. "I honestly can't believe you've never been caught. We can't just walk to Sorem's estate looking like this. We'll be spotted in no time!"

"Then how do you suggest we get there? Teleport?" replied Ari.

"What?! No! Can magic even do that?" Ronin shook his head in annoyance, when he then found his attention drawn to the numerous boxes of old goods stacked throughout the room. He stepped over to a few of them and started rifling through their contents, until a wide grin spread across his face. "I've got a much better idea..."

"Just a little further..." said Ronin with a nervous chuckle as he guided himself and Ari back through the upper-class districts of the city. His companion only offered a low growl in reply. Ronin could feel himself sweating a little, both in part from the abundantly clear aura of rage he could feel emanating from Ari, as well as his new attire. Ronin presently masked his appearance beneath a fine and hooded fur coat, the likes of which easily made him pass for a traveling merchant or other sort of successful businessman. Ari on the other hand, was now disguised beneath a far less glamorous castle maid gown, equipped with a white bonnet that was at least a couple of sizes too big for her. It was excellent for keeping her face hidden from passersby, but Ronin was even more grateful for the way it shielded him from the ferocious scowl he was positive she'd been giving him ever since they'd put on the disguises.

"Will you calm down already? Going back to Sorem's estate was your idea, and it isn't my fault that Bertram didn't have any fancy dresses lying around," said Ronin quietly to avoid drawing attention from those around them. He purposely kept them walking close to the passing street traffic; even with his and Ari's disguises, being seen alone was still riskier than in a crowd.

"I'll be calm once this whole ordeal is over with and I've beaten this memory out of your head," snapped Ari.

"Well, I guess this is what you get for guilting me into carrying your things all day. And slow down will you, it looks strange if you're walking in front of me." Ronin then grunted in pain as Ari kicked him in the leg.

"No less strange than the way you've been carrying yourself. Walk with some dignity for goodness' sake." Ronin at last scowled back at her.

The journey to Sorem's estate felt much longer to Ronin this second time around. He was used to a persistent feeling of being watched, whether it be by guards, shopkeepers, or really any random person on the streets who found his usual appearance unsettling. But all of that paled in comparison to what he felt now. He knew that Zane would spare no expense to track them down, which meant that they could very well be being followed at any given moment. Ronin was constantly sneaking subtle glances around them. He presently saw no one wearing the hunter's uniforms, but didn't rule out the possibility that some of them may have discarded their cloaks and armor to better blend into the crowds. When he and Ari finally passed through Sorem's gate, the vast and luscious greenery that covered her property almost made the place feel like a blessed sanctuary, or at least it might have if they intended to stay for all that long.

As they walked along the twisting path to Sorem's home, Ari stopped momentarily beside a small creak that passed between a few flower beds.

"What are you waiting for?" asked Ronin. He watched as Ari removed her maid disguise, and crouched down to cup some water in her hands before slashing it over her face. She then stood up and straightened her hair. Ronin shook slightly when he saw her face for the first time since they'd left Bertram's store. Ari had turned a sickly kind of pale, with dreary eyes and faded breaths. "Are you-" Ronin started to ask, but Ari just walked past him. They stepped up to the door, on which Ari banged her fist against like last time. A moment passed, but there was no answer. Ari knocked harder on the door while Ronin stepped onto the lawn towards an adjacent window and took a peek inside. Though his view was obscured by a few potted plants on the windowsill, he could still make out the clearly empty hallway and side rooms. "I think she might have gone out," he said to Ari, who ignored his suggestion and instead started to almost punch the door. "Ari..." Ronin called out worrisomely.

After a particularly loud bang on the door that must've left her hand throbbing, Ari was aggressively yanked back by her shoulder. She and Ronin gasped as they both turned around, only to find Sorem standing in front of them. She clutched a watering can in one hand and a small garden trowel in the other, though despite having clearly just partaken in her favorite pastime, Sorem's face looked anything but pleased.

"I would greatly appreciate it if you'd refrain from practically vandalizing my property. What in the world is so important-" began Sorem before stopping herself as she saw that the large backpack Ronin had been carrying during their previous visit was now missing. "My goodness... you cannot possibly expect me to believe you've just had another simple 'travel accident.'"

"Believe whatever you want," Ari said. "We... we need your help." Sorem reached a hand out and brushed it against her friend's forehead.

"Are you feeling unwell?" she asked concernedly.

"I'm just tired..."

Sorem stepped past Ari and Ronin and produced a key from her pocket to unlock the door. She motioned for them to head inside then guided them into her living room again where the two of them took seats around a small table. Sorem walked off into another room, only to return a few moments later carrying a tray of teacups.

"What can I do for you?" she asked as she set the tray down in front of them. Ronin looked to his side at Ari, as if to ask her how they should handle the situation. She looked back at him, and shared a similarly uncertain expression before turning to Sorem.

"We need information about a suspected family of witches. Anything you may know could be of use so spare no detail," said Ari before motioning for Ronin to show her the hand cloth. A little reluctantly, Ronin revealed the item from his pocket and gently laid it folded out on the table before Sorem.

The woman's eyes went wide with surprise as she gazed at the raven crest.

"This crest, how have you come by it?" she asked in clear bewilderment.

"I've had it my whole life. What do you know about it?" asked Ronin anxiously. Sorem suddenly shot up from her seat.

"This is yours?! That's impossible; to think you've been strolling through the city as happily as can be with a bounty on your head large enough to buy this entire estate several times over."

"You know of the bounty as well?! How?" Ronin also rose to his feet. Sorem looked stunned as they watched each other, and she hesitated to answer. Ronin recognized the glare she was giving him. It was the same kind of look he'd seen from Ari back in Bertram's store; a look that begged to question just who in the world he was. Ronin felt stung by this, and realized that if he were to glance at his reflection somewhere, he would likely find his own eyes staring at him just the same way.

"Many secrets come and go through my business," said Sorem after a deep breath. "Some of my clients are bounty hunters seeking potions to enhance their fighting abilities. A particularly arrogant one donning fancy armor and a dark green cloak visited a couple of weeks ago. He showed me the contract for this crest, claiming he'd need the strongest brews I've ever made for it."

"And you sold these potions to him?" asked Ari with a groan.

"I'm afraid so..." Sorem answered ashamedly.

"His name is Zane, and you mentioned a written contract," said Ronin. "Do you think he was hired specifically?"

"He couldn't have been; the contract looked mass produced. For whatever reason though whoever is distributing it is only doing so through discreet means; no public declarations or posts in taverns or notice boards."

Ronin shuddered as he listened to Sorem's explanation, and Ari pulled him back to his seat.

"If word spreads that you're the owner of this cloth, you'll have every greed crazed maniac in all of Rendolyn after you. Please, stay here. I can get you help," said Sorem.

"And who will you get?" retorted Ronin frustratedly. "If what you're saying is true then anyone with even the slightest connection to the criminal underworld could be aware of the bounty as well, it'd be a huge risk. Not to mention Zane could easily turn anyone over to his side if he simply offered them enough of the reward. I know the situation is dire. What I don't know is why any of this is happening." Sorem looked at Ronin rather confusedly.

"You truly know nothing of this crest? Or your own presumed family for the matter?" Ronin shook his head. "I see..." continued Sorem as she lifted the cloth and examined it closer, a curious look on her face.

"What is it?" asked Ronin impatiently.

"This crest... I suspected something about it back when this Zane person first showed it to me. It looks vaguely familiar, but I can't recall from where."

"Might you bring us a pen and paper?" interjected Ari. Sorem looked at her uncertainly, but went to retrieve the requested items nonetheless. She handed them to Ari and sat back down, watching intently as the young witch dipped the pen in ink and began carefully tracing it along the paper. Only when Ronin realized what exactly Ari was writing, did he finally recall that Sorem was not a witch herself, and was thus unable to see the secret arcane runes inscribed on the cloth. "This name is written beside the crest. I suspect few folks outside of this room have ever seen or heard of it," said Ari as she turned the paper around and slid it across the table to Sorem.

"Sil..." the older woman said slowly, like she was in disbelief.

"You know them?!" asked Ronin hastily.

"Saying I know them may be generous, but I definitely remember them. They were a married couple of witches that my parents did business with when I was a little girl, but it's been decades since I last heard their name."

"Did they also have a coven? Where did they come from?!"

"I... I'm not sure. It's been so long." Ronin leaned down and buried his face in his hands. "But I might be able to find out," continued Sorem. Ronin quickly shot his head up again at her words. "My family has long since kept highly detailed documents of our transactions and clients, witches in particular, stored away in our archives. It'll take some time, but we may be able to dig up some information." Ronin sighed with relief, but not quite hope. He nodded for Sorem to show him and Ari the documents. Sorem stood up again and walked off into another part of her house. When she returned, she was struggling to carry a massive pile of old papers that she promptly collapsed onto the table.

"There are several other piles to search through, and that's only if we wish to cover the last century or so at best," she said through pants. "Grab your own and start searching."

Ronin and Ari sat side by side on a cushioned sofa in Sorem's living room, tirelessly flipping through page after page of layered and faded records that seemed to pile up almost infinitely. Ronin let out a few coughs here and there as the thick layers of dust trapped between the pages flew in and out of his lungs with each breath. Many of the documents he skimmed through were hardly remarkable, consisting mostly of order forms, payment transactions, and shipping arrangements. Though an occasional few on the other hand were eerie enough to make Ronin question just how exactly Sorem's family was acquiring such information. Some pages detailed the personal information of various individuals and groups that Ronin thought may have been other witches. Things like private addresses, financial states, connection networks, and even psychological profiles flooded the papers in immense detail. Sorem's possession of this information was certainly a far more egregious example of thievery than anything Ronin was guilty of.

Disappointingly though, he found no trace or reference to his supposed family anywhere within his stack, and could now do nothing more than wait impatiently for Sorem to finish searching for more records. Ronin looked up from the papers and watched Ari as she neared the end of her own stack. He winced painfully each time she scanned through a new sheet, only to dismissively toss them one by one into the pile of documents she'd already skimmed through. He could feel what little pieces of optimism he'd been able to muster slowly burn away, until the last of it disappeared without so much as a flicker remaining when Ari finished reading her final page. Ronin was hardly surprised that things weren't going his way, but that didn't make this failure any less painful, not after the bittersweet tastes of success he'd finally had after all this time.

"Sil... Sil... Sil..." he repeated over and over in his head. He now felt very much the same way he did when he was investigating the handcloth. Stuck with a vague, directionless clue that he'd likely run out of thoughts about sooner or later. A few tears slowly trickled down Ronin's cheeks, and he found himself wishing he'd never learned his name.

"You know, I never really knew my parents either," said Ari out of the blue. "My mother died giving birth to me, and when I was a little girl, my father fell ill. He couldn't take care of me, so he sent me away to live with Jey, Elena, and the coven's previous Archwitch." Ronin turned to look at Ari, and noticed the longing frown her lips formed.

"I'm sorry..." he whispered.

"Don't be. Everyone at the coven treated me like family from the day I arrived. I never would've survived on my own..." Ari's voice trailed off ambiguously.

"What are you trying to say?" asked Ronin.

"I'm saying that I've seen the way you cower like a child every time your name is mentioned!" snapped Ari. "It's tearing you apart yet you've hardly said a word about any of it. You don't need to keep everything to yourself anymore." Ronin reeled back at her sudden aggression.

"And what exactly do I have to keep?! Much less give?" he deflected as he looked away from her again. "Before today I was a nobody traveling around with one meaningless name. Now I am the same, but with two. I see little difference."

"I know I can't force you to talk to me, but I wish you'd at least not lie to me," said Ari quietly as she raised her sleeve to his face and wiped away some of his tears. Ronin reached and grabbed Ari's wrist, wanting to push her away, but stopped. As he held her, he could feel just how much he was shaking.

"It was hardly a lie... but the truth it was not either," he muttered as he let Ari go. "I see no reason to grieve for the loss of something I never had. Call me cruel if you wish, but if my family has truly been banished from this world then so be it. I just..." continued Ronin with a grimace. "I just feel like I can't do or be anything. I can't find my family, I can't use magic, I can't build a life for myself. All I can do is run away from it all, but it's only when I run that I seem to finally come closer to the truth and I don't understand why! I don't understand why any of this is happening to me. I wish I didn't have to be Ronin Sil, or even just Ronin."

"Well... " said Ari after a moment. "As far as I can tell, Ronin Sil is a descendant of a powerful family of witches who is wanted by virtue of his name alone. Ronin, on the other hand, is a wandering rogue who would never dream of settling down with anyone, much less a coven of witches of all folk. When I dragged you from that cave, you were a complete stranger. And when we first spoke, you were quick to dismiss the significance of your belongings even though neither of us knew the true nature of the hand cloth during that moment." Ari moved slightly closer to Ronin as she continued speaking. "The person I have gotten to know in albeit a rather short amount of time seems nothing like either of those two. To me, well, you can be anyone you want to be."

Ronin froze up at her words. Once again, and in perhaps the most inconsiderate of times, he found himself unable to think of how to express his gratitude for Ari. He met her gaze despite a near overwhelming urge to hide his own, and hoped that somehow, she knew how he felt. Ari said nothing anymore, and instead continued to look back at him. In the next moment, Ari slid all the way across the couch to where Ronin was sitting, and wrapped her arms around him for a tight embrace, with her head perched gently beneath his chin.

"Wha-what are you doing?!" exclaimed Ronin as he nervously scrambled to get away from her. Ari giggled coyly at his reaction, but held him firmly as she nuzzled against his chest.

"I may be powerful, but I have no delusions of invulnerability," she said softly, and with her eyes closed. "A great danger awaits us. If this is to be my final evening, then I would prefer at least some of it to be spent in comfort." Ronin continued to shake in place, his heart beating fast, but gradually he calmed down as he accepted Ari's embrace. He slowly moved an arm around her back, and held her to himself. For a brief moment, he forgot all about his past, and for the first time in his life, got an honest idea of just who exactly he wanted to be.

Chapter Six
Confessions of Witchcraft

The inside of the estate grew dim as the evening sun slowly creeped further behind some distant hills. The living room was quiet, filled with only the hushed breathing of Ari and Ronin as they tried to stay calm. Each passing second seemed to tick by agonizingly slowly. It would be night time in about an hour, maybe less.

"Looks like we won't be making it back before dark after all," joked Ronin. Ari chuckled regretfully.

"I suppose we won't. I hope you know that if we make it back, Elena will do far more unspeakable things to you than any bounty hunter could devise."

"Well... one life threatening problem at a time, you know?"

"Indeed. I wouldn't let her hurt you anyways," said Ari as she rested against him some more. Ronin believed her.

"Ahem..." Ronin and Ari heard, followed by a few coughs. The two of them looked up to see Sorem standing in the doorway of the living room, and they quickly shoved away from each other, their faces red with embarrassment. "My apologies for interrupting..." began Sorem. "But I have some bad news." Ronin noticed how she didn't return carrying any documents this time. "We've now searched through every file my family has archived for the past half century. There is no mention of the Sil family anywhere whatsoever."

"That's okay..." said Ronin with a low sigh.

"I'm glad to hear you say that, but I'm afraid there's more to this situation. We've found no information about the Sil family, but that doesn't mean we haven't learned anything."

"What do you mean?" asked Ari. Sorem looked at her and Ronin worriedly.

"There were without doubt documents about them archived here at some point, my parents were always strict about rules and record keeping, as I am. With that being said though, there are other protocols my family designed..." Sorem gulped nervously as she focused on Ronin in particular. "In order to protect ourselves, if we ever learn that any witches we do business with are discovered by church authorities, then the rules dictate that we are to burn any trace of our affiliation with them. I can only assume that this is what my parents did with the information about your family when I was still a child."

"W-what..." Ronin stuttered slowly. He shakily rose to his feet and looked at Sorem, his eyes pleading for her to be lying to him. "Y-you're saying that the church killed my family, and is after me?" Ronin's own words faded in and out of his ears, being quickly forgotten as if they were spoken in a dream, only to echo again over and over as he tried to grasp the severity of what he was being told. Ronin had hardly managed to survive just Zane and his hunters, but he knew he stood no chance against the church. It would only be a matter of time before he was caught. "That's impossible! You mentioned no holy seal on the contract. The church is the most powerful organization on the whole continent. They have legions of their own fanatical soldiers so why in the world would they resort to unofficially hiring petty bounty hunters of all people?!"

"Propaganda," answered Ari. "In the church's eyes, their war against magic was won long ago. All that remains for them to do now is finish off the stragglers such as ourselves, but they would never publicly admit to this." Ari clenched a fist tightly in anger as she continued. "Hardly anyone believes in witchcraft these days, and the church wouldn't have it any other way. They work to ensure we no longer exist, in life, and in history." Ronin felt sick to his stomach. If the church captured any of them, it would be like they never existed.

"If the church knows who you are you'll never be able to flee from them," said Sorem. "You need to get home and hide until you can figure something out."

"We'll leave as soon as we have cover of darkness," replied Ari. Ronin listened to her voice. She was furious, and feebly trying to hold herself back. Ari had already spent her entire life locked away from the world, a world ruled by forces who would see her and those she cared about tormented until their flesh, bones, and legacies were no more than dust to be blown away into nothing- ness by the wind. Yet despite all this, she wasn't afraid of them. Ronin could tell that she'd die with tears in her eyes and a smile on her face if it meant protecting what she cared about.

"I... can't..." Ronin whispered weakly.

"What?" asked Ari as she and Sorem looked at him. Their stares terrified Ronin to his core, and he instinctively began backing away from them.

"I can't go with you..." he continued.

"What?! Don't be foolish, why not? asked Ari perplexedly as she stepped closer to him.

"Because I can't do it! I'm not like you!" Ronin suddenly shouted. "You've saved my life countless times already, but I've done nothing but drag death your way ever since you found me in that cave!"

"You yourself said that we still have a chance! The only death you'll drag by abandoning me is your own!"

Ari continued to desperately plead for Ronin to listen to her, but Ronin could hardly hear her anymore. He wanted nothing more than to stay with Ari, and desperately yearned for even the most pathetic, selfish excuse to disregard the danger his mere presence carried and go with her. But Ronin could already see heart shattering pain in Ari's eyes, and he knew he wouldn't be able to live with himself if he hurt her anymore. Ronin swallowed his despair as best he could, and turned to leave.

He was stopped after just a couple of steps though, when a strange, horrifically painful sensation suddenly overtook him. He groaned loudly and hunched over. He could feel a sharp sting in his head, like a knife was slicing through his brain, and the feeling quickly spread as a burning throb throughout the rest of his flesh. The sensation rapidly spiked in intensity, and Ronin wailed in agony as it seemingly reached its peak.

In the next moment, a ghastly array of suffocatingly dark shadows shot forth from the floor beneath Ronin. They flashed, shot, and contorted like blackened bolts of lightning, shredding through and knocking aside the chairs and tables around him before slithering their way up and around Ronin's own body, threatening to devour him whole. Ronin heard Sorem gasp in terror behind him, and did the same himself as he flailed his arms around trying to disperse the monstrous manifestations. But the shadows only continued to grow, creeping closer and closer to Ronin's face.

He raised his hands to shield himself, but a second later, the nigh otherworldly shadows flew away from him. Ronin spun around, only to witness Ari desperately trying to defuse the shadows as if they were a volatile trail of powder bombs flying around her. She reigned them in and swirled them around herself in circles, inadvertently colliding the now appendage and blade-like creations into walls and shelves before finally managing to vanish them back into the floor.

Once the chaotic shadows were gone for good, Ari stood still. Her breaths were deep, and her knees trembled relentlessly until she finally collapsed. Ronin, who had been briefly paralyzed by the intensity of the ordeal, jolted himself back to attention and leaped over to her. He carefully lifted Ari into his arms and placed her into one of the few chairs that was left standing in the room, then knelt beside her. Her eyes constantly blinked open and shut, and she somehow managed to look even paler than before, like a ghost about to fade out of the world. Ronin clutched her hand tightly. The mysterious pain he'd felt was gone now, but was replaced by sickening grief as he felt Ari's slow, soft pulse.

"What was that?!" asked Sorem as she slowly stepped over to them.

"S-spell casting... " answered Ari through fits of coughs. "It's controlled by our minds. You must have lost yours," she said to Ronin.

"I-I..." stumbled Ronin incoherently. He wanted to beg Ari for forgiveness, but instead concentrated all of his focus on calming down. If he were to lose control of himself again, Ari wouldn't be able to stop him. "She's sick. Do you have any medicine?" Ronin asked Sorem through his own gritted teeth.

"I'm afraid Ariana is beyond the aid of mere medicine..." answered Sorem sternly yet worriedly. "Rest will do her no good either at this point."

"Why?!" asked Ronin out of fright and confusion as he grew more desperate by the second. "What's happening to her?!"

"The coven..." groaned Ari as she tried to drag herself out of the chair. "Elena can help me." Her voice was weak as she fought to stay awake.

"You're in no condition to go anywhere." said Sorem as she pushed Ari back down. "As soon as dawn comes, I can fetch Elena myself. Just wait here for now,"

"Does she look like she can wait?!" retorted Ronin. "We've been here long enough as is! If we don't leave on foot tonight, we may be dragged out in chains tomorrow." Sorem opened her mouth to protest, but said nothing. They both sat in silent contemplation, trying to find any thread of hope that they could cling to. It was a futile effort on Ronin's behalf though; his mind was still so consumed by everything that had transpired over the last few hours that he could hardly even begin to think straight. This was however, far from the first time in which he had found himself in a highly intense situation where unclouded concentration was the key to survival.

Ronin closed his eyes and steadied his breathing. He briefly let his mind drift into obscurity as his senses and instincts took over.

Then, something unexpected caught Ronin's attention. A sound came from nearby. It so faint that even the heavy aura of the room may have been enough to prevent most people from noticing it, but regardless, Ronin's ears still twitched ever so slightly. He was positive that he heard a sort of light snap or creak from behind, and just as quickly as he detected it, the sound vanished.

In a flash, Ronin shot up from his knees and turned around. With a burning intensity in his eyes, he stared straight through one of the open windows. A muffled gasp was heard, followed by a loud tumble as several of the densely packed plants lining the perimeter of the house suddenly started to shake. Ronin dashed over to the front door of the estate and forced it open before jumping outside and looking towards the main gate. A short distance ahead, he saw one of Zane's hunters trying to flee from the property. The man was clearly shaken, nearly tripping over his every step as he ran, jumped, and crawled desperately through the rough terrain of Sorem's vast garden. Ronin readied himself to sprint after the hunter, but before he could even lift a foot, he was harshly yanked back by the shoulder. He collapsed down to the ground with a pained grunt. Ronin looked up to see who had tossed him aside so effortlessly, only to stare in shock as he saw Ari standing in front of him. He was in disbelief that she, who had literal seconds ago been on the verge of passing out from fatigue, could possibly be standing above him now, say nothing for having the strength to force him to the ground.

Ronin thought to call out her name, but hesitated as he took sight of her face. Ari's eyes were wide open, their blue tint glistening just the same as the first time he'd seen them, though now they possessed an unwavering, blink-less, nigh feral glare that she aimed directly at the man ahead of them. Her entire body trembled as if ready to shatter at any given moment, but she didn't seem to care. It was like she'd experienced some bizarre spike of energy, and all that presently existed in the world to her was that one cowardly man. Ronin recoiled back nervously; Ari looked terrifying to him.

"Stay... away... " she growled without looking at him. Her voice carried a sinister, yet desperate tone, like those two small words alone had consumed the last bits of self-control she had left.

As the fleeing hunter neared the gate, Ari, much to Ronin's surprise, didn't give chase. She simply watched him from where she stood. The hunter made it no more than a few yards away from the still sealed gate, when Ari finally raised one arm, and with a burst of renewed power, grabbed onto the large shadow cast by the gate itself. She then yanked her hand back, causing the gate's shadow to massively expand and blast towards the man like an avalanche of darkness. The horrified ranger shielded himself with his arms and started to scream, but was silenced almost immediately as he was swallowed whole by the monstrous entity. For a few seconds, the dark tide stormed over the poor man. When Ari finally released the shadow, he was left lying on his back, groaning heavily and coughing up blood before soon becoming unresponsive. Ari then started to slowly limp her way towards him.

"Ari..." Ronin called out weakly as he watched her from his spot on the ground; she ignored him. Ronin slowly pushed himself to his feet. "Ari?" he called out again. He anxiously started to follow her, but stopped in his tracks once she arrived at the collapsed hunter. He wanted to help Ari, but at the moment she seemed like some wild creature that would attack if he provoked her. Ronin watched as Ari knelt down by the hunter's side. She shakily raised a hand towards his head before aggressively yanking down his hood to expose the man's face. As it turned out, the person she revealed could hardly be considered a man. He only looked maybe a year or two older than Ronin or herself at most.

"Ronin!" came a wild cry from behind. Ronin shot his head back to see Sorem stumbling out of her house. She had a large bruise on her head and clung to the open door for support. "Stop her!" Sorem pleaded as she tried to make her way over to them as fast as she could. Utterly confused, Ronin turned back around again, only to reel back in shock as he witnessed what had just begun to happen. Ari had placed one hand on the man's forehead to hold his head upright, her nails clawing into his skin from how tightly she was holding. With her other hand, she grabbed him by the chin and forcefully wrenched his mouth open as she moved to lean her face over his own.

In the blink of an eye, without any hesitation whatsoever, Ari descended on him, practically biting his mouth with her own. Paralyzed by shock, Ronin could only watch helplessly as all of a sudden, the man's throat, mouth, and face alike, all began to glow vibrantly with a mysterious, unnatural orange and blue hue. As the glow grew brighter, the man's eyes pried open again, as he was abruptly roused from his unconsciousness.

Near instantaneously, the man let out a muffled wail at the top of his lungs, his suffering so hellish and clear that the mere sound of it left Ronin trembling and nearly collapsing to the ground. The man raised his arms and aggressively started pushing and punching Ari wherever he could, but she absorbed each blow as easily as a faint gust of wind. Eventually, the hunter's limbs and body began to flail and convulse erratically as his tormented shrieking continued. He fought desperately to escape from whatever bizarre and inhuman torture Ari was mercilessly causing him, but after a few short seconds, his struggles started to grow weaker, and he passed out again.

Once the hunter stopped resisting, Ari lifted her face ever so slightly away from the man's, finally giving Ronin a clear glimpse of what was happening. She moved her fingers to purse his lips, and did the same with her own. From his mouth into hers traveled a narrow stream of an eerie, orangish blue, mist-like substance that she seemed to be sucking right out of him. Ronin couldn't believe that he was watching the same sweet, caring girl who had rescued him on more than one occasion. Whatever Ari was doing looked nothing like shadow magic, and it was killing the poor hunter painfully slowly.

Ronin grunted and stumbled forward as he felt something collide against his back. He looked ahead to see Sorem limping past him, but she paid him no attention as she chased after Ari, begging her to stop all the while. Ronin grit his teeth hard, buried his fear as deep as he could, and then charged forward. He didn't know what was happening, but he knew he needed to do something. Ronin quickly overtook Sorem, and reached a hand out to try and lunge for Ari. Before he could grab her though, Ari fired one arm back in his direction, sending forth a devastating blast of shadows. Ronin raised his arms to brace himself against the attack, but the shadows smashed into him like cannonballs, sending Ronin flying back until he slammed against the ground and tumbled even further away.

The attack wasn't fatal, but it left Ronin severely bruised. He tried to get up, but could only manage to prop himself up with his elbows and look ahead at Ari, who continued to consume the mysterious glowing mist like nothing else mattered to her. Every instinct Ronin possessed, every cruel and cold lesson he'd learned in life, every shred of common sense for survivability that even a child would have, all pleaded for him to flee from Ari. But Ronin forced such thoughts out of his head like they were the naive and delusional ramblings of some madman he'd met during his travels. He didn't want to be that person anymore.

"Ari!" Ronin screamed as loudly as he could.

Nothing existed for Ari. The grass beneath her feet, the wind drifting through her hair, even the voices of her friends from moments ago had all passed away like soft drizzles in the aftermath of a great storm. All that was left now... was bliss. And in her mind and flesh, it was the purest, most unfiltered kind of happiness anyone could ever imagine feeling. It came from nothing, no grand accomplishment nor gain, but that didn't matter, for there was nothing for Ari to think about. No thoughts drifted in or out of her head; there was just a pleasant, peaceful silence. Ari felt like she could stay this way forever, as if she was impossibly safe from all of the pain, chaos, and cruelty in the world.

This feeling persisted for what felt like a lifetime, until something started to pick and poke away in the back of Ari's head. She felt a faint, tingling sensation spreading over her. It was annoying, like an itch she couldn't scratch. Ari tried to ignore it, but the longer she waited, the stronger the invasive feeling grew. A vision then flashed in her mind. It was dark, and only lasted for a fraction of second, but a moment later it flashed again. Then it happened again, and again, over and over until it felt like she was rapidly blinking at a painting. She fought against the surreal image, but whether her eyes were open or shut, it quickly became all she could see and perceive. Then, Ari recognized what she was seeing. The dark, claustrophobic image that flashed before her was the cave she'd discovered Ronin in. She felt a sharp pain in her heart, and in that moment, her ears erupted with the sound of her name being shouted.

Ari's eyes opened wide, and she at last realized what she was doing. With a terrified shriek, she flung herself off of the young hunter. She frantically crawled back, but couldn't quite bring herself to look away from him. The man was a complete stranger to Ari, yet she still stared at him with a morbid sense of recognition. In her eyes, the man's face seemed to slowly blur out and fade into obscurity; transforming from a unique individual into a blank slate or template of a human being that instead looked all too familiar. Ari shakily rose to her feet, tears now streaming down her cheeks as she stared at the man from above. Her face lay partially hidden behind her disheveled bangs, but they couldn't hide the guilt and grief that were consuming her. Ari felt a sense of devastation and self-loathing so profound that it had to be far more prevalent in the sick fantasies of sadistic torturers as opposed to reality. Her eyes, however blurry their vision was, fought hard to deny the truth in front of her. She'd lost control of herself again, and the price was yet another life. Ari let out a ghastly scream, and buried her face in her hands, her nails viciously raking down her forehead and cheeks. It should have hurt tremendously, but Ari felt almost nothing.

The sickly paleness her skin had possessed mere moments ago was gone now, and in this regard, Ari felt better than ever. The newfound strength in her blood and bones fought like a rabid horde against her will, forcing every drop of her pain into her heart and imprisoning it there. The confined grief was so volatile and conflicting with the renewed vigor Ari was feeling. It was like perpetually being on the tipping edge of a total mental and physical breakdown that would ultimately never come.

As Ari held her face tightly, she noticed how eerily quiet everything around her had become. There were no more screams nor cries; all that remained was a grim standstill. Ari turned away from the man, and reached up to clear her eyes and brush her hair out of her face. She looked ahead, silently hoping that all she'd see would be an empty abyss, and that is when she saw him.

Resting on the grass ahead of her, propping himself up on his elbows, was Ronin. He was trembling in place, and looked ready to collapse from pain, exhaustion, or downright shock. Ari didn't know what exactly he was thinking or would do, but when their eyes connected, one thing was made abundantly clear. He was deathly afraid of her.

The look on his face pushed Ari over the edge. She felt her heart explode, only to have all of that suffering still be trapped in place by the walls built by the power she'd stolen. Without so much as a word to Ronin, Ari turned around, smashed her way through the gate, and ran away.

"Ari..." Ronin called out again, but only in his head as she disappeared behind the gate. That last scream had caused him to lose his voice, and he coughed violently for a few seconds while massaging his throat. Ari may not have seen it, but Ronin was also crushed when she ran. He was on his own again, back to lying in the dirt, and he couldn't even say it was to protect her anymore. Ronin forced himself to stand. He coughed some more and held

his aching head tight. He heard a soft moan come from behind him, and turned around to see Sorem painfully pushing herself off the ground. Ronin rushed over to help her. He tried to urge Sorem to lie down and rest, but she brushed him aside and stood up regardless.

"You... you stopped her?" asked Sorem. It was clear that every word she spoke pained her greatly, but she still uttered each one with dire strictness. She needed to know.

"I-I don't know what I did. She ran away." Sorem moved past him and limped her way over to the motionless hunter. She and Ronin knelt down next to him, and Sorem ran her fingers along his neck to feel for a pulse.

"He's alive!" she exclaimed with relief. Ronin reached down to feel for himself. The pulse was incredibly weak, but with hasty treatment, he might survive. "I know a doctor who lives close by. I'll get him taken care of. Don't worry, with enough coin I can make it so that the truth of his injuries stays buried."

"Have you gone mad? This man was trying to get us killed!" said Ronin. "We have to focus on helping Ari-"

"He must live!" snapped Sorem. "Please, if you really want to help Ariana, then trust me. I'll deal with this man, but you have to find her before she is caught." Ronin hesitated at her words. He knew without doubt that he wanted to find Ari before Zane inevitably did, but at the same time he couldn't deny how much the thought of confronting her terrified him.

"W-what did she do to him?" Ronin pleaded to know. "What is she?!"

Sorem released the man and turned to Ronin. She placed a hand on his shoulder and stared him in the eyes.

"She's Ari," answered Sorem confidently. Ronin shook beneath her grasp, but nodded silently. He pushed her hand away as he stood back up and headed towards the gate.

The streetways through Meadow's Peak were more or less familiar to Ronin by this point, but the lively yet secure sensations that the humble city usually gave off now felt far more twisted and conniving than he was comfortable with. It was like every road, alleyway, or side path were all just individual threads composing a massive spider web ready to alert its predatory inhabitants at any given moment.

The day had gone cold and windy, and by now the bright orange coloration from the late evening sun had descended into layers of shade and gray that covered and obscured all that could be seen. This of course posed no serious issue to Ronin in and of itself given his effective night vision, but as the prolonged darkness of night ticked ever closer, so did the busy activity of the streets come to a finish, along with Ronin's hope of being able to blend into any crowds. Thus, the paranoid feeling of being watched he had experienced for the last few hours only grew stronger with each passing minute.

Ronin hurried his way through the streets and back towards the market as inconspicuously as he could manage despite still being in an immense amount of pain. He hoped that with that scout incapacitated he would at least have a little time before Zane tracked them down again, but regardless, he needed to find Ari quickly, and he had only one farfetched hunch as to where she might have gone.

When he returned to the large market square, he found that it now bore almost no resemblance to the way he was used to it appearing. The loud ramblings of vendors and customers alike had been replaced by the echoing footsteps of a mere handful of business folk pacing around as they closed up shop. Ronin looked to the other side of the market and saw that the doors to Bertram's store were shut tight now, and not a single light shined from within. Meadow's Peak might as well have become a ghost town.

Worry grew within Ronin as he pressed on, and the brisk speed walk he'd approached the market with evolved into an exhausting jog up the hills of the city. Quiet and empty roads, chilling winds breezing past his face, dangerous pursuers, having no certain destinations or plans in mind, these things were all second nature to Ronin; cold realities of life that for the longest time had lost any sense of right or wrong to him. But for now, he refused to accept any of them no matter how much fate pressured him to. Ronin followed the road halfway up the hill then quietly peeked around a corner. Straight ahead of him was the small bridge Ari had taken him to earlier, and just as Ronin had hoped for, Ari was right there. She sat by her lonesome atop the thick stone railing of the bridge. Her red hood was raised, and her legs dangled over the edge, swaying ever so slightly in the nightly breeze while she looked towards the darkened horizon as the last few rays of sunlight waved goodbye before vanishing behind the hills in the distance.

Ronin was hesitant to approach or call out to her, for fear that if she noticed him, she may simply run away again or worse. Instead, he just watched her from afar. He wasn't able to see her face, but he heard no cries, and she was holding as still as anyone ever could. It was clear to Ronin that there was far more to Ari's life than he ever could have imagined, and he looked at her with worry. What he saw was an enigma, uncertainty, the kind of which likely posed more danger than nearly any other individual in the world. But what he did not see and had never seen, was clear. There were no boiling cauldrons, cursed dolls, or devilish rituals anywhere. Despite the secrets she was hiding from him, the last week he'd spent with her had still broken every preconceived notion of a witch Ronin had thought he knew. There was just a girl sitting before him now; just Ari.

Ronin swallowed his fear, and started walking over to her. He made no effort to hide his presence anymore, and was surprised to find that Ari paid him no attention even as he got close to her. She had no way of knowing if it was him, Zane or one of his hunters, or even just some random stranger who was approaching her, but she didn't seem to care one way or another. Ronin stood but one step behind Ari now. Her presence carried a grim aura of hopelessness that felt familiar to him. Ronin could easily picture himself sitting where she was now.

"We don't have much time..." he spoke softly. "I don't think Zane knows where we are. If we go now, I can help you sneak out of the city."

"We can't escape," said Ari. Her voice was plain and devoid of emotion, and aside from those few words she did nothing to acknowledge him. It was like she was barely even there.

"I know it's risky but I still think-" began Ronin before being interrupted.

"We can't escape because I can't leave. I cannot return home nor run anywhere else. This has to end now." Ari's voice cracked a bit as she continued speaking. "I have to be stopped."

"What you did to that man... that was no shadow magic... "

"No, it wasn't..." muttered Ari weakly. "I lied to you. I lied when I said that witches aren't evil. I am the most vile monster imaginable." There was not a single hint of doubt or exaggeration in her voice. Ari truly believed that about herself.

"W-what do you mean?" asked Ronin. His legs twitched instinctively, but he rooted his feet in place. Monster or not, he needed to know the full truth.

"Most folk need only food and water to survive, others medicine and care, but I... I feast on their souls. And I savor every second of it." Ari words trailed off her tongue with an almost sinister tone that left Ronin's skin crawling.

"I know you're scared," Ari continued as she started shaking in place. "You were right though, the plan could still work, for you. Go." The way she told him to leave was cold and unwilling to negotiate. It reminded Ronin of the way he'd been banished from his final orphanage once he came of age.

"Well of course I'm scared!" he snapped in a whisper. "An hour ago, I wasn't sure if souls or whatever you're talking about even existed, and now you're saying you need to take them from others to survive?! Why Ari? Why must you do this?"

"You assume I know?!" Ari snapped back as she finally turned to face Ronin. "How could anyone ever understand such unnatural evil forced upon them against their will? As if it were something as simple to comprehend as the flowing of water or the setting of the sun. It is a horrific curse that I may have been born with for all I know, a birth that I lament more with each passing day." Ronin sighed sorrowfully as he listened to her. Spontaneously, he grabbed onto the railing, and not so carefully hoisted himself up to a sitting position beside Ari. Ronin took but one small moment to flinch nervously as he saw how far a fall from here would be, then swiped the worry off like a bug. Ari turned to Ronin out of surprise. "What?! Go back fool! You need to escape-"

"Have you really spent your whole life sheltered and naive enough to think you're the only person who despises the way the fate of this world has treated them?" asked Ronin unsympathetically as he looked off into the distance. "Whenever I was chased by those who wanted me dead for one petty reason or another, I sometimes genuinely wondered why I was bothering to run? Even if I did escape, to what end would it serve? Where would I go? What would I do? And who would I be with? The answers were the same every time. Nowhere, nothing, and no one." Ronin paused, taking a second to collect himself. "I can't in good faith try to sell you on hope, because the truth is that I honestly didn't have a reason to keep running, I just did it anyway. But you're different Ari; you have reasons to run, people to run to."

Ari was trembling beside Ronin, so much so that he worried she might accidentally slip off the railing. He was shaking too. Ari opened her mouth to respond but could only slur her words over one another incoherently at first. She silenced herself, and took some deep breaths.

"How can you say that after what you saw me do? I couldn't control myself Ronin, I could hurt you."

"I can't imagine it would hurt any more than just leaving you here to die."

"And you call me naive... Perhaps you are right, but this isn't a matter of reason. That hunter may have been our enemy, but it wasn't just him. I've hurt a lot of innocent people... I don't deserve to go on."

"He's alive." said Ronin. "The scout you attacked. He survived; you stopped yourself at the last second." Ari looked at Ronin, her eyes wide with disbelief.

"I... how could that be true? My mind was gone like always. I felt nothing, I cared for no one."

"You're stronger than you think," answered Ronin. "Whatever happens when you lose control... that isn't you. You're not a monster, and you sure as hell don't deserve to die like one."

Ari looked down and said nothing at first, as if she was contemplating her decision.

"You're coming with me," she finally said.

"Only until you're out of the city-"

"To home. You get no say in this." She sounded just as non-negotiable as before.

"If I do that, you might not have a home for long. And what about Elena and Jey?"

"We're a family, and you're one of us now. They'll want to protect you." Ronin had to do a double take in his head of what Ari just said. He couldn't decide if him being 'one of,' pretty much anything was nonsense or not, but at the same time, he realized he'd never know for sure if he didn't listen to her.

"Alright," he conceded. "We go together." Ronin lifted his legs and slid around in his seat, attempting to stand back up, but Ari held him back with a hand on his shoulder.

"Before we go, there's one more thing I need to know..." she began. "You didn't have to come after me, Ronin. Why do you care so much?"

Ronin shook at her question; the answer was difficult for him to confess.

"That cave you found me in, I was awake in it for some time. I did not know where I was or what was happening, but after realizing that I was stuck I... I didn't try to get free. I gave up until I passed out. I gave up because before you saved me that day, I had never met anyone so kind." Ronin turned to see Ari's face, but the wide-eyed look she was giving him made him more afraid than any all-powerful spell or curse could ever hope to. He tried to turn away again, but Ari reached a hand out to his cheek and stopped him. "And I was starting to think I never would."

Chapter Seven
Beneath a Blackened Sky

Ominous clusters of darkened clouds blew in slowly from the east, periodically blocking out the gloomy moonlight for short moments here and there, and rendering the city beneath it all a blinding shroud home to little more than wind howls and cricket chirps. Conditions for a night such as this used to be seen as bad omens by the folk of ages past; a time when other worldly spirits would roam the streets and infest the nooks and crannies of homes in envy of those still lucky enough to be alive. Ronin thought back to what he had asked Ari on the road; if these childish fairy tales truly had any merit to them. It was quite ironic that discovering the existence of magic only furthered his uncertainty of nature, and a part of him thought it might actually be somewhat convenient if a mob of ethereal spirits stormed the city now of all times. He knew this wouldn't happen though, but not because the possibility didn't technically exist in his still mostly ignorant imagination. In Ronin's eyes, a lifetime of hazardous misfortune and unrelenting apathy from those around him had finally ended when the world gave him a second chance in the form of the companion now by his side, and he severely doubted that even the slightest stroke of good luck would ever grace him again.

Presently, he and Ari quietly stood next to each other around the corner of a small household that rested along one of the backstreets of Meadow's Peak that led towards the eastern gate, a direction Ronin figured would be less predictable for them to go as opposed to the southern gate they entered from earlier. Ronin's back was pressed firmly against the outer wall, with Ari nudging against his side. Her breaths were quiet but strenuous, and Ronin could feel her body shaking against his own. The game of cat and mouse was second nature for Ronin, but despite technically having been hunted for her whole life, Ronin could easily tell that Ari was far less comfortable living amidst the constant possibility of a blade suddenly swinging out from around a corner, or an arrow flying from across the street at any given moment.

He turned to see Ari's face beneath her hood, and made eye contact as he rested a hand on her shoulder, as if to tell her that she needed to relax and stay focused. Ari took a long breath and nodded to him. Ronin then turned back and ever so slightly peeked his head around the side of the building and into the street to survey their surroundings. The view was crystal clear to Ronin, and he smiled to himself at how powerful the night made something as simple as sight feel to him. This ability definitely would've helped avoid more close calls than he could remember over the years. He took a thorough glance at everything from the wide roads and rooftops to the claustrophobic alleys that lay scattered between the buildings. There were no signs of activity whatsoever, in fact everything before his eyes held so perfectly still that the city almost looked like a painting.

It was still unknown to them just how many men Zane had at his disposal, and Ronin could only hope that the number was small enough to make monitoring and patrolling the city an unreliable strategy, in which case they would most likely be watching the exits from inside or outside the walls. Nevertheless, he still was not foolish enough to risk traveling in the open when they didn't need to. Ronin turned back to Ari and signaled that everything looked clear. He then stepped past her and gestured for her to follow him as he guided them both through the alleyways bordering the street. They moved as quietly as they could, but even the slightest thump or crinkle from their footsteps was enough to cause stress. After a while of making their way towards the edge of Meadow's Peak, Ronin saw the walls of the city straight ahead. He carefully glanced from the cover of a building again, and saw that the gate was closed as expected.

Ronin looked to the ramparts above; dropping down from the top of the wall would be their only way to escape the city. Climbing the side of the wall like last time would be difficult for him to do quietly, and likely impossible for Ari to do at all, which left the stairs by the gate as their only option. Spaced out in relatively long intervals on the wall were small beacons of light, emanating from the torches of a couple of guards as they made their rounds across the perimeter. Getting caught by even one of these guards would not only give away his and Ari's position, but would likely end up with their imprisonment and interrogation for trespassing. Ronin rolled his eyes as such a thought occurred to him. It always seemed that law breakers and law makers alike were both equally out to get him, a contradiction that Ronin had never been able to fully rationalize.

He patiently observed the guards' patrol routes for a moment, and just as the man nearest to the rampart Ronin had his eyes on started to move away, he grabbed Ari by the hand and started to discreetly approach the stairs. They carefully ascended the steps, and Ronin pleaded with whatever forces came to mind that the creaks of the wood beneath their feet would be drowned out by the distance. When they arrived at the top, Ronin estimated that they had around thirty seconds before the guard turned around and started making his way back to their position. All that remained was to drop and then make their way south towards the safety of the tree line. Their situation was manageable, but even the slightest mistake could bring disaster. Ronin turned to Ari to make sure that she was watching him closely, and proceeded to quietly vault over the edge of the wall. He spun around as he did so and hung by the edge as he dangled his legs towards the ground to minimize the fall distance. He looked back to Ari again and nodded at her to copy his movements. She cautiously heaved herself over the edge beside him, and held on tight. She looked down, and then back at Ronin nervously. He matched her gaze.

"One, two, three!" he mouthed silently, then dropped down to the ground.

The soft grass muffled Ronin's careful landing, but Ari's drop didn't go as well. Her feet landed hard, causing her to lose her balance. Ari collapsed to the ground, and tumbled loudly down the hilly terrain until she smashed against a large rock. Ronin fought hard to suppress a worried gasp, and quickly rushed over to her side. He rolled Ari over so that she was facing him, and was relieved to discover that she was mostly okay save for some minor bruises. She struggled to stifle some grunts of pain, and Ronin held a hand over her mouth just to be safe. He helped hoist her back to her feet, then they turned towards the forest in the distance. They slowly started walking away from the city, but stopped after just a few steps as a loud voice called out to them from behind.

"Stop right there!" shouted someone from atop the wall. Ronin and Ari turned around to see one of the guards waving a torch in his direction, and froze as he saw that the man was carrying a deadly crossbow with his other arm. "Bloody smugglers again. If I see you so much as sneak a glance away from me, you'll have a bolt in your head faster than you can blink." Hearing the noise, the guard's fellow watchman quickly hustled over. "Open the gate and bring those wretched bandits back inside," ordered the first guard as he lowered his torch and took a precise aim of his weapon directly at Ronin's face.

Ronin began to panic internally as he listened to the sounds of the second guard's boots stomping their way down the stairs to the gate. He felt at a loss for options. Attempting to flee and dodge the guard's shots would be an all or nothing gamble, and one rigged near hopelessly against their favor given his vantage point and their lack of cover.

"We're not smugglers." Ronin called out. "Please... we've nothing of value on us and we just want to go home." In Ronin's experience, attempting to reason with an angered guard was an exercise in futility akin to the likes of trying to sail a boat up a waterfall, but he had to try something. He couldn't let them fail here, not when they were so close.

"I'm sure the city dungeon will look just as pretty as whatever sewer trench you call home," retorted the guard. Ronin tried to protest again, but his voice was drowned out by the hulking creaks caused by the eastern gate of Meadow's Peak as it was slowly dragged open. Ronin felt Ari grab ahold of his hand tightly. He heard her weakened voice whisper a soft apology. He winced to himself, and in that moment the crossbow pointed between his eyes was the only thing that prevented him from snapping at her for trying to take the blame. In the absence of a strategy, Ronin's mind was running rampant with fumes of shame as he rapidly recollected every aspect of the escape plan he'd been formulating since the afternoon, and chided himself for not being able to do better. The decisions he made were the only things he ever had any control over, and for once, he felt that the consequences brought by them truly mattered.

They remained at a standstill. As foolish of an idea as it sounded in Ronin's head, their only chance to escape without Ari using her powers would be to jump the guard as he came to apprehend them, and hope that the other man would not fire with his fellow soldier in the way. Ronin waited patiently, tuning out all noise around him, and concentrating all his focus on listening for the guard's footsteps as he approached the two of them. But as time continued to tick by, Ronin was met with a surprise. He didn't hear any footsteps at all, in fact he heard practically nothing. The gate was fully open now, and the silence persisted for a moment longer until the guard above grew aggravated.

"For the lord's sake Theo! What's taking you so long?!" he shouted, only to be met with no response. The guard grew angrier and more stressed out by the second. He shot a quick glance over his shoulder but could not see his partner anywhere. He shouted into the air again, and his trigger finger twitched precariously, causing every hair on Ronin's body to stick up straight.

A second later, a pair of arms suddenly appeared behind the guard, looking as if they had been spawned from the depths of the darkened night itself. One arm immediately wrapped around the neck of the guard in a choke hold, while the hand of the other clasped itself over his mouth. What had started as a split-second gasp from the guard quickly devolved into a fit of feeble squeals as he viciously struggled against his attacker before soon going limp. The guard collapsed down, leaving Ronin to stare in horror at the toothy, satisfied grin of Zane who watched them from above.

Their exchange of looks lasted mere seconds. As Ronin recognized that the confrontation he had been so desperate to avoid was now threatening to both begin and end in an instant, so too did he realize that by incapacitating the guard, Zane had inadvertently given him and Ari the initiative. He could still feel Ari's hand clinging to his own, and without any hesitation, he spun around and made a mad dash across the fields outside of the city. His aggressive movements yanked Ari along with him, and a renewed feeling of panic generated energy fueled their haste. The fields were long and empty, but right within their view up ahead was the dense tree line of the forest. Their night vision combined with Ari's knowledge of the rough terrain would give them an enormous advantage over Zane, if they could just make it there.

They ran relentlessly, without so much as a single glance over their shoulders. Ronin could hear the trampling of Zane's pursuit not far behind them, but it was soon interrupted by a high-pitched humming sound of sorts, like a bird's call. He looked back mid sprint to see Zane perching a small whistle between his lips, and blowing into it incrementally he chased them alongside a couple of other hunters. The noise traveled far in the dead silence of the night, and Ronin looked around to dreadfully witness that many more hunters were mobilizing across the fields in the distance, and rallying to their leader. All in all, he counted roughly twenty or so of the Darkwood hunters all rapidly closing the gap created by his and Ari's meager head start. Their attackers all started to let out a series of ferocious cries as their boots pounded over grass and rock; the hunt was on.

The clouds began to move past the moon, and the remaining darkness of night, much to Ronin and Ari's dismay, provided little assistance for the time being. Zane and his men moved faster than they did, and were thus able to keep sight of their targets all while Zane continued to blow louder and louder into the whistle to signal their location to the rest of his troops. Ronin picked up his pace as much as he could and urged Ari to do the same. They hadn't been running for all that long, but the intensity of the situation still rendered their blood boiling and their lungs begging for air as they soon reached the small hill that gave way to the edge of the woods.

They could see the trees just up ahead. To anyone else, such a sight would appear as little more than a twisting wall of blackness through which a leaf could hardly be distinguished from a branch. But Ari and Ronin on the other hand, were able to see deep into the heart of the woods as far as the masses of tree trunks would allow them. They were only a handful of yards away from the woods, when Ronin saw a strange, ball shaped object fly over his head and crash into a bush. A second later, the area of the tree line around where it had landed exploded in a roaring blaze of fire. Ronin leaped back out of fear and shock, tackling Ari down to the ground by accident as the two of them harshly collided. Ronin turned around on the ground, and saw Zane clasping another fire bomb tightly in his hand, with about a dozen other bow wielding hunters standing beside him. Ronin grabbed Ari again and tried to get up, but they were both forced to recoil back down when their ears were pierced by a ghastly howling noise that rapidly drew closer.

A split second later, a volley of deadly sharp arrows landed several feet to their left. They attempted to flee towards the other direction but out of the corner of his eye, Ronin saw the archers taking aim again, as a few more hunters continued to charge at them. The strange arrows screamed like banshees as they soared through the air, intimidating Ronin and Ari into staying down. The second volley cut them off just as the first had. The fire behind them now provided perfect vision of their position. Ronin knew that Zane would prefer to capture him alive, but he was not about to try and call him out on a bluff by running straight through the lethal firing zone in front of them. He began to panic; he didn't know what to do. Out of every time he had been chased, none of his would-be attackers came even close to matching the relentless skill and tenacity that Zane and his hunters were currently displaying. Ronin was snapped back to his senses when he suddenly received a harsh shove to his back that pushed him away. He looked behind himself, expecting to see Zane looming over him like a reaper, but was surprised to find that it was Ari who had forced him away and was now firmly holding her ground in the face of their overwhelming enemies.

She stood tall, and though she was visibly shaking, Ronin could see that her face refused to show Zane any fear. She closed her eyes and breathed deeply; her arms rested plainly by her sides. Ronin forced himself back up from the ground.

"Ari?! What are you doing?!" he shouted at her, desperate and confused. He shot an arm forward to try and grab Ari's shoulder, but his hand was quickly swatted away as Ari aggressively flicked both of her arms upwards. In the next blink, Ronin was left stunned as a massive sea of shadows blew out of the ground in front of Ari. The spell roared thunderously into the air, like boulders tumbling down a mountainside that drowned out the noise of all other commotion. The monstrous entities swarmed everywhere around them, circling each other repeatedly to create a hulking cloud that devoured Ari and Ronin. The massive manifestation of shade expanded further in all directions, even soaring into the air like smoke from flames powerful enough to destroy a whole city. The veil of mist was darker than the night itself, and Ronin knew that any ordinary person attempting to gaze through it would question if they'd gone blind. He watched as the wave of charging hunters closest to them stumbled back, before fleeing in terror only to have the shadows storm over them. This was their chance.

Ari kept the spell up for as long as she could, but was eventually forced to relent. She lowered her throbbing arms, and turned to look at Ronin over her shoulder. She was panting heavier than he thought possible, with streams of sweat trickling down her face in the aftermath of that certainly draining spell. Still though, Ronin could perceive a glimmer of hope and pride in Ari's eyes, a glimmer that was quickly replaced by a pained gasp, as another volley of arrows struck through the remnants of the shadow cloud, with a single one managing to pierce straight into Ari's side. Her eyes went wide as the pointed head of the arrow skewered through her flesh, and she fell for one moment that to Ronin, seemed to drag on for an eternity until he heard her body crash onto the grass with a muffled thump. Ronin wanted to scream, but could only wheeze in disbelief as he yanked himself over the ground to Ari's side. He knelt next to her, all color instantly draining from his face as he watched her lie motionlessly on the ground.

"Ari?! Ari?!" Ronin shut his eyes and grit his teeth hard, hoping to wake up from a terrible dream as his despair turned to rage. In that moment, he wanted nothing more than to yank that arrow out of Ari's side and charge suicidally with it at Zane until either or both of their blood stained the fields. He reached down and grasped the arrow shaft, but stopped himself when Ari suddenly let out a feeble cough. Her eyes fluttered open and shut, and Ronin watched her, torn between relief and horror. She was alive, but needed help fast.

Without hesitation, Ronin snapped the arrow shaft and scooped Ari up in his arms. With the remains of Ari's slowly dissipating spell covering their escape, Ronin turned towards the tree line, and sprinted forward, leaping over the dwindling flames while carrying Ari, as the two of them finally escaped into the forest.

Twigs snapped and leaves crunched beneath the fatigued and disorderly tramples of Ronin as he forced his way through the dense thicket surrounding him. His aggressive movement over the rough terrain was anything but subtle. Every now and then Ronin could hear the sounds of various night creatures scattering away into the distance. Worrying about whether or not they would end up giving away his position wasn't something Ronin could presently afford to stress over. Ari was losing blood; hurrying was all that mattered. In fact, it seemed that all his hope rested on the possibility that Ari's spell had simply stopped Zane and his men in their tracks entirely. Despite everything he'd learned over the past few days, the power and spectacle of magic never failed to leave Ronin's jaw hanging, so surely Zane must have been affected ten times worse, he reasoned.

Ronin had been running for some time now, taking rapid glances over his shoulder every few seconds to see if Zane was still giving chase. He never once caught sight of his foe, which left Ronin undecided as to whether he should feel relieved, or even more on edge if that were somehow possible. He only had a vague idea of what direction the coven was in, but he'd search all night if that was what it took to get Ari home safely. Ari's arms and legs dangled down, swaying back and forth like wind chimes in the nightly breeze that was accelerated by Ronin's sprint. He did his best to hold her head up. 'All night,' was likely well outside of Ari's dwindling time. Minutes or hours may have passed as he ran, Ronin couldn't tell. He was drenched in his own sweat, and his muscles threatened to tear like worn out fabric at any given moment as his energy gradually withered away. He didn't want to admit it, but he knew he was beginning to slow down. The tension and exertion he'd endured throughout the night, combined with now having to carry Ari was getting to be too much for him whether he liked it or not. He attempted to dash around a large tree, but stumbled when his foot got caught on a root. He fell forward, and barely managed to avoid collapsing on top of Ari by balancing himself with a kneeling position.

Ronin gasped for air, and attempted to stand back up, but only rose a few inches before collapsing down again, his knees feeling weaker than mud. He surveyed the forest around them, but could feel his eyelids being dragged down by the stress of his own fatigue. Even to him, the night forest was now beginning to look dark.

"Ronin..." he heard faintly from below. He shook himself to attention, and looked down to see Ari, her eyes struggling to stay open much the same as his own. "Put me down..." she whispered. Ronin scowled at her.

"I promised I'd get you home," he said. Every word he spoke caused a thrashing pain in his chest as they dragged more air out of his lungs in their battle to escape his lips, but Ronin spoke them anyway. He held her even tighter, and finally pushed himself back to his feet, as he started to limp and jog onwards.

"Put... me... down," Ari mumbled again.

"You don't get a say in this!"

"I-I want to run with you." Her words echoed in his mind as his pace quickened.

"I want to run with you too." And Ronin meant it. No matter the odds, he wanted to run with Ari to the end of the world, and then some further.

Some distance later, Ronin found himself standing in front of an especially dense thicket that branched off to both sides as far as he could see. He turned to his side to shield Ari from the many branches and leaves, and pushed through them with his shoulder. He fought the brush as if it were another hunter, and nearly made it through when he suddenly lost his footing at the tip of a small hill. He slipped forwards, dropping Ari by accident as the two of them rolled down the hill. Ronin's face landed in a filthy pile of dead leaves, and he groaned in pain. When he raised his head, he saw Ari lying on her back a couple feet ahead of him. She was groaning as well, her breath far more faded than his own, but she was awake still. Ronin began crawling over to her, but paused shortly as the rest of their surroundings came into focus. Not too far ahead, past another layer of plants that nearly obscured his view, was the coven.

Ronin smiled painfully, feeling relief for the first time all night. He finished crawling to Ari, and threw her arm over his shoulder before pulling them both up.

"We made it, Ari! We made it!" he said as cheerfully as he could, hardly being able to believe his own words. No lights emerged from within the building, but the long walkway through its courtyard still called to them as if it were the lone path to sanctuary within the deepest chasms of the underworld.

Ronin could feel Ari repeatedly sliding further down his side to the point where she was almost kneeling on the ground, but he heaved her back up each time.

"Help!" he screamed towards the coven. He coughed heavily, and had to hold still for a moment. His throat had already felt like he'd chugged boiling water, and that last desperate plea had only made it worse. He swallowed his own spit, wishing it would turn to water, and prepared to shout again, but before he could, the front door of the coven quickly flew open.

From inside emerged a bright aura of light that rapidly approached him and Ari. It hurt nothing more than Ronin's eyes, which he shielded with his free hand out of reflex. Still though, he snuck a few painful blinks through the cracks between his fingers, and saw Elena and Jeremiah rushing over to them. Jey was the first to arrive. He dimmed the light as he knelt down beside them, and practically yanked Ari from Ronin's grasp and rested her against himself. He looked her over, and gasped when he saw the arrow head still embedded in her side, her own blood mixing in with the red fabric of her cloak.

"Wha-what happened?!" he asked while looking at Ronin, his loud voice riddled with worry.

Ronin wanted to tell Jey everything, but he was so exhausted he could hardly say a word. He rested on his knees before them, and held his chest and throat.

"Hunt-" he started to spit out, before being interrupted as he found himself aggressively grabbed by his upper body. He was then dragged a short distance away from Ari and Jey, and painfully slammed onto the ground on his back. His vision was hazy, but he looked up to see Elena leaning over him and holding him tightly by the shirt. She stared at him without blinking, her face trembling much the same as her hands that shook Ronin alongside her. The rage spread across her face looked stronger than any kind he'd ever witnessed before. He felt frightened, but when a few tears streamed down her cheeks and dripped off her chin, falling onto Ronin's own face, he swore he could feel the pain in her heart eating its way through his skin. She wasn't just angry, she was afraid.

"What did you do to her?!" she shouted loudly enough to nearly deafen Ronin.

Ronin winced in Elena's grasp.

"I'm sorry..." was all he could bring himself to say to her. Elena screamed again, and slammed her open palm down on the grass beside his head. A burst of lightning exploded upwards from the ground, creating a blinding flash that briefly lit up the area around them in a white haze before the bolts disappeared into the sky.

"El... " came a voice from behind the two of them. The call was soft, but repeated a few times until Jey shouted for Elena's attention. The hysterical archwitch shot her face backwards to be met with the sight of her friends desperately reaching out to her. She released Ronin, and dashed over to them.

"She's losing blood. I'm taking her inside!" said Jey as he lifted Ari up. As he started dragging her towards the coven, Ari reached out a hand and rested it against Elena's arm.

"It's not his fault... " whispered Ari." He saved me... help him, please." Elena raised her own hand, and rested it against Ari's firmly for a second, before gently pushing her away.

"Inside. Now," she ordered before turning back to Ronin.

Ronin was beginning to get up again, when Elena grabbed him by the upper arm and yanked him to his feet.

"You owe her your life again!" she snapped while dragging Ronin towards the coven. "This is your one chance to explain yourself."

"Bounty hunters... " Ronin began. "They're after me."

"Bounty hunters?! That's absurd!" exclaimed Elena. "Why in the world would... " she continued, but her voice was quickly drowned out in Ronin's mind.

His attention was now tunnel focused on one thing entirely. The rays of light reflected by the moon managed to discreetly snake their way down through the foliage above. In the distance, a shining trickle of this light descended betwixt the many leaves of one of the larger clusters of plants that lay beyond the courtyard. There, Ronin spotted a small twinkle resting firmly. It sort of resembled the reflection of a coin or mineral, but Ronin knew it to be neither. It was a sight that had been previously unfamiliar to him until the moment he had miraculously recognized his night vision, but one he could never soon forget after the fact. The small glisten ahead was none other than that of an eye.

Ronin dreadfully leaped backwards, but quickly turned to sweep their surroundings much to the confusion and stress of Elena. His heart skipped a beat as he realized what was going on. Hidden amongst the vegetation, scattered in a wide semi-circle around the four witches, were a horrifying number of human faces all menacingly peeking out through their hoods. And his recognition did not go unnoticed.

Ronin expected a series of battle cries at any moment, but all he heard instead was a frustrated groan and the shuffling of bushes as a lone figure emerged from the center of the enemy's position.

"If only I had known that the biggest source of our headaches would come not from our target himself, but from the pitiful woodland sprites he shields himself with," called out Zane as he stood with arms crossed frustratedly. Elena turned to face him, and Ronin could hear Ari and Jey stopping in their tracks behind him. "A lot of painful irony could've been avoided. Truly Ronin, I expected you to be far more than just another gutter rat. Still though, I thank you for at least being an excellent guide. Four witches are a much greater prize than just one." Ronin felt like a massive weight had been dropped over his shoulders as the grim realization sunk into his mind. Zane uttered the word witches so knowingly and carefree, as if the people he was referring to were as ordinary as farmhands. Zane was no ordinary bounty hunter; he was a battle-hardened witch hunter.

"The bounty is for me alone. They've done nothing to you!" Ronin called out while gesturing to the three other witches around him.

"They're monsters. Sure, we want to butcher them, but they wish to do the same to us normal folk. The key difference is that with the right opportunity, they could slaughter thousands in the blink of an eye!"

"But-" began Ronin when he felt Elena pull him back by the shoulder and step forward.

"He's exactly right," she said as she snapped her clenched fist open, conjuring a volatile ball of lightning above her palm. "The blink of an eye..."

Zane flinched ever so slightly at Elena's aggression, but quickly brushed it off, then smirked as if she were no more than a child wielding a butter knife.

"You glorified cultists think yourselves to be so powerful, fooling around with the elements as carefree as you can be," continued Zane before turning his attention back to Ronin. "You know Ronin, the pay for your capture is truly staggering, and worth twice as much if brought in alive. I only ever see that kind of coin from bounties of a more... personal nature."

Zane's last comment caught Ronin's attention. It was obvious that Zane had previously claimed many similarly under the table bounties to hunt other witches, but now he was claiming that the church was willing to pay far more for Ronin specifically, or rather the supposed last surviving member of the Sil family.

"What are you saying?" asked Ronin as he stepped forward. Zane didn't answer him though, and instead just grinned in satisfaction.

All of a sudden, Ronin felt a hand clasp around his mouth, as his left leg was swept away, causing him to be tackled to the ground. Ronin shook and struggled as hard as he could to try and free himself from his ambusher, and through his muffled screams and grunts, he could hear the same cries coming from the others as they were all overpowered around him. The hunter attacking Ronin moved his other arm around Ronin's neck and squeezed tightly, making it impossible for Ronin to breathe. Ronin could feel himself starting to go faint. With their capture now all but assured, a surge of emotions and desperation overwhelmed Ronin. Fear, sorrow, and regret burned his heart with a searing pain that felt not unlike the kind in his air deprived lungs. His hatred for Zane was swiftly matched only by that which he now held for himself, as he realized that his distraction had given Zane's hunters enough time to outflank them.

Amongst all of Ronin's despair though, was something else. Another sensation lingered about, a feeling that Ronin could hardly recognize, as for most of his life prior to this day, he'd decided that it was pointless. Ronin was outraged. Outraged that this was the final destination that all of the branching paths in his life had at last led him to. His fury grew in strength, and with it came a haze of visions. Images of Ari, Elena, Jey, and every other kind soul he'd met recently flashed in his mind.

"*Please...*" Ronin pleaded. He didn't know who or what he was asking for help. Just something; anything. Ronin ceased his struggling, and could feel his mind and body going numb. He let out one final, muffled scream.

A thunderous whoosh was heard, like the winds of a great storm, as a series of powerful shadows spawned out from the ground in a wide area around Ronin. The man who held him, as well as a couple of other nearby hunters, shrieked as the appendage-like manifestations collided with them, and sent them flying away into the forest. The hunter restraining Elena released her, as he and what remained of his nearby comrades all began to flee while attempting to evade the dangerous shadows. As she gasped for breath, Elena spun around on the ground and shot a powerful blast of air over her friends, straight into the backs of the retreating hunters. The attack sent them soaring forward, with many of the hunters slamming into solid tree trunks with enough force to break through some of the smaller, thinner ones as the cracking sounds of snapping trees mixed in with the crunches of shattered bones.

Ronin held still on the ground, and the aggressive shadows he'd accidentally conjured vanished just as quickly as they'd appeared. That spell had been even stronger than the one he'd experienced back at Sorem's estate, and for the first time, Ronin was beginning to personally feel just how draining such spells could be. He attempted to drag himself towards Ari and Jey, but could hardly move a muscle, until he saw Elena rush over to him and grab him by his upper body as she dragged him the short distance to the others.

Their victory was short lived though, when through the darkness, Ronin watched the rest of the hunters that encircled them raise their bows. Elena was the only witch still standing, but her back was turned to the archers.

"Behind you!" Ronin called out to her, but his weak voice was drowned out as another loud, whistling howl rang through the air when the archers let loose their volley. Being defenseless against the attack, Ronin shut his eyes tightly. He expected the sting of the deadly sharp arrows to pierce his flesh immediately, but all he perceived instead was a loud clinking sound, as if the arrows had collided with solid stone. Ronin opened his eyes again, and saw that a luminous orange bubble now surrounded him and the others. Through its transparent walls, he watched as Zane ordered his hunters to fire again. Another wave of arrows soared forwards, only to slam into the bubble, their heads shattering as they violently ricocheted off the bright surface.

Ronin heard a strenuous grunt, and looked behind himself to see Jeremiah on his knees, gritting his teeth hard as he held his arms high, the glowing shield emerging from his open palms.

"Fry them already El!" Jey screamed. Elena turned around to face their foes again. A short distance ahead a smaller group of hunters had drawn their swords and were now charging at the shield.

"Left side!" Elena called out. Jey seemingly knew exactly what she wanted to do, as he immediately opened a small hole in the shield beside Elena. Ronin watched as the archwitch pointed her hand forward, and blasted a devastating blast of lightning at the hunters. The crackling bolt struck one of them in the chest, and with a single pained howl, the man was knocked down to his back, where he lay motionlessly as thick fumes of smoke emerged from the seared remains of his apparel. The rest of the advancing hunters all either ducked to the ground for cover or turned to run. Elena fired bolt after bolt at as many of them as she could, until she yelped in pain as an arrow flew through the hole in the shield and grazed her cheek, sending blood oozing down her face and some sliced strands of her hair swaying down to the ground.

Jey immediately sealed the hole in their shield. The spell itself looked impervious to the hunters' attacks, but the arrow fire was relentless, and each consecutive volley seemed to weaken Jey's decaying strength. Elena turned towards the tree line again, preparing to return fire on the archers. She readied another lightning bolt in her hand, but hesitated. She first looked left, then to the far right, before quickly shooting her view every which way, her previously calculated gaze having devolved into a frantic search.

"I can't see them! I need a light!" The archers were much farther away, and Elena didn't have Ronin's night vision. To her, it must've looked like the arrows were being fired by the dark blur of the night itself. A loud thumping sound was heard in between volleys, as a few dark, ball shaped objects struck the shield and bounced to ground nearby. Ronin hardly had time to gasp when the space in front of Jey's shield exploded in a bright, blazing inferno. The flames from the bombs spread quickly, devouring the many stray plants and dead leaves that littered the ground, their strength crashing against the shield like a battering ram.

"Ack!" cried Jey as he tried desperately to hold back the raging fire, the bright orange hue of the shield beginning to fade and flicker. The pain of maintaining the spell was enough to knock him on his back. "I can't!" he shouted to Elena.

Ronin painfully forced himself to a sitting position just in front of Elena, and looked ahead. After having stared through nothing but utter darkness all night, the sheer brightness of the fire scorched his eyes perhaps as much as it would his skin, but he looked through it anyways. Ronin could see that Zane's hunters maintained their semicircle formation with strong discipline. Knowing that mere men could challenge such powerful witches was in and of itself enough to make Ronin tremble. But he could also see the archers' quivers begin to run low, their pockets and packs go empty. He'd already seen some of the hunters scream and rout, Ronin had even caused some it himself. They had to be shaking too. In the center of the hunters' position, Ronin glimpsed Zane. The young witch hunter leader was barely visibly, being mostly hunkered down in cover behind a large rock, not even looking towards at Ronin at the moment. Despite his advantage, Zane was worried, Ronin assured himself.

"Ten o'clock, thirty feet ahead!" he called out before turning to face Elena and Jey, who looked back at him uncertainly. "There!" he screamed, pointing in the way he'd mentioned. In perfect tandem, Jey created another hole in the shield right as Elena fired a lightning bolt in the target direction.

An agonizing wail echoed throughout the woods as the bolt landed with a direct hit onto one of the archers. His companions nearby shook with visible dread as it was made clear that their cover was blown. With Ronin's careful guidance, Elena mercilessly fired more lightning at the revealed men. Several more were quickly shot down, shattering the morale of the rest of as they started to flee. Every hunter that abandoned their assault made the arrow fire that much less powerful, and the lingering flames begin to dwindle as they quickly chewed through the many small leaves and plants they'd ignited. As the pressure on the shield eased up, Ronin heard Jey exhale profoundly, as if a bone crushing weight had been lifted from him, and the shield suddenly flared with power.

Victory was near at last. Ronin aggressively turned to face what remained of the Darkwood Hunters. He opened his mouth to call out more targets for Elena, but hesitated at the last second, and fell silent.

"Ronin where are they?!" screamed Elena after a couple of seconds, but Ronin said nothing to her. Something else had caught his attention. Straight ahead, he saw Zane again, only now he was rising from behind his cover and openly moving towards Ronin and the others. The remaining hunters strangely stopped attacking as their leader advanced. In his hands, Zane tightly clutched the strange star shaped necklace Ronin had seen earlier. Ronin could see his lips moving, as if Zane was muttering something, then all of a sudden, Zane started shouting an ominous, unknown chant into the air as he raised his necklace high.

"Twelve o'clock!" Ronin called out, and the crackling of another lightning bolt quickly drowned out Zane's voice. The woods flashed brightly again, only this time, the light remained. A near blinding orb of glowing white light emerged from Zane's necklace, as if its twinkling star had just fallen from the heavens and landed in his hand. Elena's lightning bolt fired towards Zane and his bizarre conjuration in an instant, but no cries nor thumps of a body crashing to the ground were heard in the second that followed. As quickly as the spell had been cast, it disappeared.

Ronin trembled on the ground; he looked over his shoulder to Elena, and saw her shaking like she was just as stunned as he was. Elena fired another bolt at Zane, then another, but each time they were reduced to no more than an echoing hiss as they passed into the unnatural glare cast from Zane's necklace, and were devoured by it. After a few more attacks, Elena fell to one knee, gritting her teeth hard as she tried to force herself back up to no avail. She seemed ready to pass out entirely. Those last few spells must have been painfully more exertive to cast than any others.

Ronin slowly dragged himself over the ground to try and help Elena, but he wasn't alone. With his necklace still held high, Zane began marching towards the shield in plain view of Ronin and the other witches who cowered within it. With each tread, Zane's boots sent the lingering embers from the fire on the ground soaring into the air. He now stood but a few short feet ahead of the shield. Zane stared through the barrier at first, and Ronin timidly looked back as their eyes met. The young rogue did what he could to try and hide the fear that his face and body language were practically screaming, but his efforts were hopeless. Ronin couldn't hold back his emotions this time, not when he was surrounded by the only people who'd ever fought by his side.

Ronin groaned as he rose to his feet, and stepped in between Zane and the others.

"You're only after me..." Ronin pointed out again. As he spoke, Ronin realized he didn't even want to hide anything anymore.

"Even if that were still true, you just killed half of my men." Zane's voice was mostly plain as he spoke, but Ronin detected a hint of genuine anger as he uttered these words. "Surrender now, and I promise to bring you in unharmed, but regardless, a debt must be paid..." Zane nodded towards the other witches behind Ronin. Ronin winced visibly at Zane's words, his hands shaking as he tried to restrain himself from lunging at the hunter. Zane smirked at Ronin's reaction, his confidence still just as bloated as ever.

"Before this is over... will you at least stop hiding for just one second?" asked Ronin.

"What in the world is that supposed to mean?"

"It means you can't fool me anymore. You walk over here tall and smiling, but only to make an offer? With sweat streaking down your face and your body twitching ever so slightly beneath that cloak nonetheless? That grin is a lie; you're afraid, and I can see it clear as day." Zane paused briefly, then let out a heavy sigh.

"You know Ronin, if you weren't so naïve, you'd probably be a far better bounty hunter than I am." Zane's voice sounded somewhat humble for once. "I honestly don't know if you're right, but suppose I just tell you what you want to hear, what good would that do anyone? Do you honestly think that the most successful, powerful people in the world are the ones who are honest about who they are? No..." Zane stepped back, and carried his necklace across his chest until he held it just above his shoulder. "They're just the ones who wear the best masks."

Zane then swiftly swung the necklace in a large arc in front of himself, and in an instant, the orb it created seemed to surge with energy as it sent forth a blinding wave of white light that slammed against the shield. Ronin couldn't cover his eyes in time, and he immediately felt a burning pain in them, like someone had stuffed hot coals beneath his eye lids. He stumbled around, and through his now blurry and double vision, saw Jey, who had fallen on his back and was shrieking in pain as if Zane's attack had struck him directly. Still though, Jey held his arms high to maintain the shield, blood oozing out of his nose all the while. Elena wasn't doing much better, being collapsed on her side as she slowly crawled over to her friends. Behind himself, Ronin heard Zane uttering that same mysterious chant from before. He turned around and saw Zane down on one knee, clutching his necklace tightly against his chest. The light orb had grown dim in the aftermath of Zane's devastating attack, but the more the hunter chanted, the brighter the light became once again. Ronin limped forward, wanting to rush Zane while his guard was down, but as he did so, the arrow fire from the other hunters resumed.

Ronin turned back in a panic; he doubted Jey's shield could withstand another blast. His distorted gaze slowly traveled down, until for the first time since he'd gotten back to the coven, he looked to Ari. She was lying on the ground a short distance behind Jey, and was holding so perfectly still that she didn't even look alive. Ronin forced his way over to her as quickly as he could, nearly tripping in the process. He arrived alongside Elena, and knelt next to Ari before carefully lifting her into his arms.

"Ari? Ari?!" Ronin called to her. Ari's lips remained still, but the weakest flutter of her eyelids was enough to give Ronin hope.

"She needs energy!" Ronin said as he turned to Elena. "She told me you could help her." Elena flinched as if she were trying to understand how Ronin could possibly

241

know that about Ari, then rested her palm against Ari's cheek while slowly tracing her hand down her face and neck.

"She's too far gone..." Elena said sorrowfully.

Ronin felt a throbbing ache in his chest as he listened to Elena. He clung to Ari tighter, and leaned forward so that his face was hovering right over hers. Even if their lives weren't already at stake, Ronin could never accept what Elena was telling him. Not when there was still one thing left he could do.

"Take me!" Ronin said, hoping Ari could hear him. "Take my strength!"

"What?!" cried Elena. "Ronin she's too weak to restrain herself! She'll kill you!"

"No, she won't!" retorted Ronin. "Listen to me Ari, you said that to you, I can be anyone I want. Well, who do you want to be? Your curse doesn't control you, you're so much more than it!" Ari's eyes opened slightly. She was still unable to speak, but a lone tear sliding down her cheek was enough to tell Ronin how she was feeling. Her expression was painful for him to look at. Ronin closed his eyes, and leaned down some more until his forehead was pressing against her own.

"It's okay..." Ronin said to her. "It's okay." And with that, Ronin gently pressed his lips against Ari's.

Ronin felt nothing right away, but after this faint moment of hesitation, the same mystifying orange and blue glow spawned in his throat, shining brightly enough to further illuminate the dim ground below. It traveled quickly, like wind through a meadow, from Ronin's mouth into Ari's; from his life into hers. Ronin then felt a scorching, unnatural amount of pain erupt within himself. It felt as if his guts were being melted by lava. He screamed torturously, and lasted only a few short seconds before instinctively trying to pull away and free himself from this agony. Ronin went nowhere though, as when he tried to yank himself back, he realized that Ari had reached her arm around behind his head, and was now holding him tightly in place with iron grip that seemed to be rapidly growing stronger.

Ronin's own strength was drained away just as quickly. He was forced to cease his struggles as most of the feeling in his body disappeared. Ronin collapsed in Ari's grasp, his vision dimming as his mind went numb, all while he did his best to concentrate on nothing other than simply staying awake.

The sound of Zane's chanting soon came to end, and with it, the forest was once again set ablaze by the powerful radiance that emerged from his necklace. The young hunter rose from his kneeling position, his legs shaking the tiniest bit as he did so. Perhaps it was from a shimmer of worry, but regardless, Zane raised his necklace to his shoulder again, and swung it outwards without hesitation. A second tide of glittering white light blasted forward from his star styled relic. The flare was relentless in its rapid charge forward, until it crashed into the weakened remains of Jey's shield. In less than a second, the orange barrier that surrounded the witches was finally destroyed, shattering into many glass-shaped orange fragments that quickly disappeared into the air. In that same miniscule instant though, a different force emerged from within the remnants of the shield; a colossal and overwhelming body of shadows.

The shadows roared like thunder, and crashed effortlessly over the light wave, swallowing it into their purely dark void as no more than a small speck as they seemingly sought to consume the entirety of the forest. Zane didn't even have the time to gasp nor brace himself before the shadows stormed over him. The blast knocked Zane over, and he grunted in pain as his body crashed against the ground with a loud thump. He was still conscious though, and groaned while forcing himself to a sitting position. Zane briefly rubbed his face, then lowered his hands. His jaw dropped out of terror as he stared at what now surrounded him, or rather what did not.

The forest, the courtyard, even the lingering embers from the ground had all disappeared, alongside any sight of his remaining followers or foes. All that was left in their stead, spanning outwards in every direction, was a suffocating, depthless, and utterly horrifying void of dark emptiness. Zane wondered if he was dead; he couldn't picture this place as being anything other than a grim afterlife, but the rapid beating in his heart told him otherwise. Panic set in right away, and Zane began waving his arms around, desperately hoping to find something, anything tangible that he could cling to aside from his own body.

Zane screamed out of stress and rage, then knelt down as he held his necklace tightly. He began his chant again, only this time he spoke much louder and faster, stumbling over his words here and there, and flinching each time as if to curse himself in his head. When he finished, the star necklace shined brightly again, and Zane screamed for it to vanquish the darkness that imprisoned him. The light erupted from the necklace, but to Zane's dread, it simply vanished into the void like a matchstick tossed into the ocean. Zane quickly repeated the chant to try again, but just before he could finish, an appendage-like shadow suddenly snapped loose from black ground beneath him. It coiled its way around the star dangling from the necklace like a snake, before aggressively squeezing itself together. A loud crunching sound was heard as the star was shattered. Zane winced painfully as several of its fractured shards stabbed into his hand.

Zane fell back to a sitting position; he couldn't bring himself to scream again, and just panted on the ground. He stared ahead into the darkness and closed and opened his eyes repeatedly, each time seeing no difference, until eventually, something started happening to the wall of shadow in front of him, something that made him want to hide. A small segment of the wall broke at first, separating into many tree branch shaped pieces that all twisted and contorted before pulling away from each other. The end result was a door-like gap in the shadows, through which Ari entered.

Her dark hair blended in almost perfectly with the void around her, but her pale skin and blood-stained clothes stood out clearly.

"This is the world you drove me to..." Ari whispered menacingly, her soft voice still echoing clearly in the absence of any other sound. She and Zane were all that existed here now. Ari knew this, and it infuriated her.

"Wretched w-witch!" stuttered Zane. His hood had fallen back, revealing the entirety of his face which was clearly no longer able to hide how afraid he was as he sat there on the ground like a cornered animal. Zane quickly drew a small knife from within his sleeve, and attempted to throw it at Ari, but as he raised his arm, a shadow quickly spawned from the ground beside Zane and restrained his wrist.

"I'd love to let you try it, believe me," said Ari, who made no effort to conceal her anger. Ever since their confrontation back in the alleyway, Zane's face had become the embodiment of everything Ari despised about the world. Every wicked piece of propaganda, every night she spent hiding away, every witch that had fallen before today; she wanted to blame Zane personally for all of it, regardless of whether or not that even made any sense. Yet now, even with her foe cowering beneath her feet, Ari felt no sense of satisfaction or justice.

Despite his success as a witch hunter, Zane was still hardly even a middleman in the war against magic; a mere pawn of pawns, perhaps less. His defeat would at best mean returning to her old life as if this day had never happened, but that life now started to feel like a fading memory, and one that she couldn't bring herself to try and hold on to. What Ari had done to Ronin made her sick. She was angry and wanted revenge, but even more than that, she was simply tired. No matter what the next day might bring, she just wanted this night to be over, but there was still one thing left that she needed to do.

"Where would you have taken us?" Ari asked.

"W-what?" said Zane as he chuckled perplexedly. "After everything that's happened, you're seriously stopping to ask questions? Go read the bounty contract if you're so curious; I'm sure you can salvage a copy from multiple of my dead men." Zane then flinched in pain as the shadow restraining his wrist tightened like shackles.

"I don't want to believe that there's any individual out there who has hunted more of my people than you have. Tell me more."

Zane hesitated at first, but then took one more look at his 'surroundings,' before turning back to Ari, a conceded scowl having overtaken his face.

"These witch hunting contracts always say to bring the targets to the nearest thieves' guild house, but that's just a façade. Every time we show up, a nameless man with a face so unremarkable you might not recognize even if it were your own always sends us to some isolated location; a cave, abandoned house, something like that. Inside is always the same thing too: a box of coins and a note telling us to leave the targets." A lingering impression of frustration and disturbance emanated from Zane's tone.

"And then what?" pressed Ari.

"And then nothing; nothing ever happens. No one ever comes to collect the targets. After the first few bounties I couldn't resist being curious. Time and again I hid in the trees and waited, but after hours, even days not a single soul ever appeared. But eventually, when I'd go and check on the targets, they'd just be gone. And without so much as a drop of blood left on the floor to remember them by. It's like they never even existed."

Ari shuddered at Zane's words.

"T-that can't be true! You must know more!" she said.

"All I know for certain is that if you prove your worth, they eventually make the job easier for you." Zane then waved around the string that remained from his necklace. "If you don't believe me, then why not go check for yourself? The nearest thieves' guild is just a few days away in Solaris."

Ari paused. It wasn't that she didn't believe Zane, in fact she could easily see the church happily orchestrating such insane schemes if it meant hunting witches. She just simply wished he was wrong. Ari rested one hand against her other arm, holding herself softly. She was real, and only she could decide who or what she was. She'd known this idea for a long time, but could never really feel its meaning. Until tonight.

"Do you regret it?" Ari asked.

"What?"

"Hunting witches. You chased me and Ronin all day just to end up here: inside the same kind of nothingness you wanted to condemn us to. So, after all that, do you finally regret what you've done?" There was no malice or anger in Ari's voice this time, just a longing hint of desperation. She truly wanted him to be sorry, even if she knew he wasn't. Zane sighed, and though he was still shaking, he stared Ari in the eye as he spoke to her.

"I first discovered that witches actually exist almost three years ago. Since then, I've seen many abhorrent things: nightmarish beasts summoned to tear people apart, fires powerful enough to combat lakes, and many other horrors that frankly make a lightning bolt to the chest seem merciful. And now this," Zane said while gesturing around them. "Can you honestly tell me you've never done something so awful to someone before?" Ari said nothing back to Zane, but the way she painfully winced in remembrance was enough of an answer. "I knew it. I may be a murderer, but you're a monster."

Still holding herself, Ari stepped away from Zane with her head hung low and her eyes tearing up. She took a deep breath, and then a second later, shot her arms upwards. Zane shielded himself reflexively as the shadowy prison Ari had created followed her motions, its dark walls all soaring upwards, at last revealing the battle scared yet eerily silent and empty remains of the forest around them. The shadows converged in the sky, forming one pulsating, heaping body above. This entity was given relative view only by the twinkling starlight that encircled it; it looked like the world's darkest storm cloud had appeared above the forest.

With one hand still holding the shadows in the air, Ari pointed behind herself to Elena and Jey, whose weary faces were torn between worry and relief as they both held on to an unconscious Ronin who currently looked pale enough to pass for a withered spirit.

"These are my friends!" Ari shouted as Zane watched fearfully. "They've never harmed an innocent soul. To them, and to all of the kind, compassionate people in this world like them, who are courageous enough to not just kill what they don't understand, I am no monster!" Ari paused momentarily, catching her breath through gritted teeth, before continuing in a low yet ominous voice.

"But to you, and to every evil murderer like you... I'll gladly be your demon." And with that, Ari lowered her arms, and the blackened sky came crashing down.

Epilogue

The cawing of crows from their nests in the tall trees above rang through the air incessantly, like a city's tower bell signaling to all that a new day had begun at last. In truth, both of these noises irritated Ronin to no end, or at least they did on any ordinary day. On this fresh autumn morning however, the sound was somewhat pleasant. Today marked the third day in the aftermath of his and the witches' perilous fight for survival against Zane and his hunters. Or at least that's what he'd been told. After having his most of his life force sucked out of his body through a proverbial straw, Ronin had been unconscious until the following evening, and it had taken an extra day of rest entirely for his strength to begin recovering. His recollection of that night was hazy, but his memory of the burning pain he'd felt during that decisive moment with Ari still lingered clearly like a scar branded on his flesh.

While he didn't regret his actions, such an experience was undoubtedly one Ronin hoped he'd never have to repeat. And besides, the pain was not alone. Ronin breathed a pleasant sigh as Ari's words from back at Sorem's estate echoed in his mind.

"To me, well, you can be anyone you want to be..." If Ari could conquer such a mysterious and horrible curse, then surely he could at least build some kind of name for himself. Ronin chuckled softly; that was perhaps the most optimistic thought he'd ever had.

These past few days had made for some of the quietest times Ronin's life. Ronin, the traveling rogue who estimated that he only ever had a prolonged conversation with another person less than a handful of times per year. Aside from the others briefly filling Ronin in on what he'd missed, hardly a word was spoken by anyone. In some ways, the silence reminded Ronin of how things had been when he'd first begun staying at the coven. He'd felt the hours tick by from the privacy of his room, only ever being interrupted by the occasional footsteps of someone passing through the halls outside. It wasn't as if he, Ari, Elena, and Jey had nothing to discuss now though, quite the opposite in fact. It just seemed as if no one knew where to begin, or was ready to face the reality that was staring at them all now more than ever.

Life at the coven had been safe enough for a long time prior as far as Ronin could tell. Too safe, perhaps, which made Zane's attack a grim reminder of why witches had to hide in the dark places of the world. Staying hidden was, in some sense, the best 'victory,' they could realistically hope to achieve, even if said victories rarely earned them little more than time. Time in a world that no matter how powerful the magic possessed by a witch was, simply no longer welcomed them. The awfully dense vegetation of the forest creeped around the coven like a besieged castle's walls. True victory would only come when they could all go to sleep with the sights and sounds of a fair summer's meadow in the distance. Or even just a neighbor's house, Ronin felt.

And that conclusion is how Ronin found himself where he was now, standing all by his lonesome with a hastily made travel pack slung over his shoulder, right at the edge of the coven's courtyard. He had his back turned to the place, and stared remorsefully at the metaphorical road ahead as feelings of guilt and grief began to consume him. In all his years, he had never known what it felt like to truly call a place his home, and now he couldn't even be welcomed into someone else's without bringing his own burdens with him, and in the most literal sense imaginable. It was a cruel, yet not particularly surprising kind of irony for his life, he felt.

With tears welling in his eyes, Ronin took his first step off of the stone floor of the courtyard, but paused as he heard a leaf crunch beneath his foot. He had never cared much for the sake of others before, or even himself for that matter. In his mind, his decisions had almost always been fueled by a meaningless, instinctive need to carry on. Right now, though, Ronin wanted more than anything else to be selfish, but his consciousness would not allow it. The hunters weren't going to stop coming for him, so Ronin figured the least he could do was take his problems away with him, so to speak. He couldn't risk endangering Ari and the others any more than he already had. He owed them that much, at least. Ronin swallowed his despair, and started walking away. The long and lonely road was one of the only places he knew anyways, he thought to himself.

"Hey, I think you forgot something!" a voice from behind suddenly called to him. Ronin regretfully turned around to see Jey approaching him, carrying one of the magic books Ronin had been reading in his room.

"Oh, um, that's okay. I don't need it anymore," he answered.

"Well then would you at least be polite enough to put it back on the shelf?" teased Jey as he lightly punched Ronin's arm. "Going somewhere?"

"Yes... I just figured it was time to hit the road again," responded Ronin uncomfortably.

"Oh please, don't tiptoe around the subject with me. With a bounty on your head so large I've half a mind to capture you myself. Admit it, you're going after whoever is out to get you, am I correct?"

"I guess you are... "

"Spill it then, what's your plan?" Ronin hesitated, realizing now that his impulsive decision to leave hadn't left much room for planning.

"Well... Ari and Sorem say this bounty has church backing written all over it, so I guess that's where I'll start." Jey laughed at Ronin's words.

"Good grief you must be joking, right? I mean I knew you were naive but I never would have guessed you to be downright suicidal. One wandering idiot with a knapsack, against the single most influential organization on the entire continent. Surely you must be insane?" Ronin cringed with a mix of embarrassment and worry as Jey pointed out the exact ridiculousness of his situation that he had been so desperate to avoid thinking about for the time being.

"It's something to do," he answered with a shrug. "I should at least be able to find out more about these witch bounties, which according to Zane, means a trip to the nearest thieves' guild holdout."

"That place could be packed with other hunters after you though. Sounds like a fast way to get caught, no?"

"No one besides Zane's group has seen my face, and with any luck the rest of them will still be searching for some filthy, rag wearing alley rat," Ronin said as he tugged as the sleeve of his fresh clothes.

"Hm, good point. Said alley rat was also traveling alone though, right?" asked Jey.

"Um, yes. Why?"

It was at this point that Ronin noticed that Jey himself was also carrying a small travel pack.

"What's that for?" he asked while pointing to it.

"Oh, this thing? It's just filled with a bunch of necessities and personal items. The rest of us figured we can't really stay here anymore either," answered Jey rather nonchalantly. Ronin frowned, feeling terrible that he'd forced them to come to such a decision.

"So where will you be going then?" Ronin asked timidly.

"I'm not entirely sure at the moment. Our exact destination has been left rather vague." Jey's answer confused Ronin. "Look…" continued Jey as he rested a hand on Ronin's shoulder. "Elena will likely never admit this to your face, but you know that there are no hard feelings, don't you?"

"How can you say that?" replied Ronin. "I almost got you all killed."

"Well, I suppose that may be true, but it wasn't really your fault honestly."

"But if we had never met, then you, Elena, and Ari wouldn't have gone through any of this."

Jey was about to say something when the two of them were interrupted by a loud noise coming from inside the coven. They looked back across the courtyard to see the front door of the building be blasted open by a huge cloud of shadows that also sent Archwitch Elena tumbling to the ground ahead of it. Her groans of pain were muffled as her face had landed in a bag of her own.

"My point exactly," said Jey with a chuckle before running over to help Elena up.

Ronin now stood by himself again, his heart pounding with anxiety as he listened to the heavy footsteps coming from within the coven, which soon gave view to the visibly outraged Ari, who also carried a bag as she stomped her way over to him.

"Let that pain be a reminder that while you are indeed the archwitch, you are certainly not my mother, and I will go wherever I please, with whomever I please!" shouted Ari as she passed by the still dazed Elena.

"And you!" she pointed to Ronin while drawing closer to him. "I am left in utter disbelief at how forgetful you can be of our score. You have rescued me but a mere three times now, whereas I have saved your life on at least five separate occasions. You needn't worry about me when any and all danger in the world is clearly far more severe for yourself!" As Ari arrived in front of Ronin, he could see in full detail just how offended she was that he would even dare to imagine wandering off on his own again. He braced himself in preparation for her verbal or perhaps even physical lashings, but was left stunned as she said nothing more, and instead just grabbed him tightly by the arm and continued walking towards the big world ahead.

Ronin was still shaking, but as he was pulled along by Ari, and could hear Elena and Jey walking not far behind them, he smiled softly to himself. Ari really did never settle.

Afterword

Before I say anything else, it's essential that I get the most important component of this parting speech done first, and that of course has to be expressing my limitless gratitude for my artist and dear friend. Magic is definitely real, and it occurs when one sees the creations of their imagination brought to life in such immaculate detail. I still get the biggest smile on my face every time I look at any of the art pieces for this book, and I doubt that will ever change. You did far more than simply draw for me though. No matter how afraid or close to giving up I ever got, you were always immediately there to smack me across the face and tell me that I have what it takes to get this project done, and that is something I will always remember. From the bottom of my heart, thank you Stef. You are the most incredible person I've ever met.

I spent a long time standing right at the edge of the finish line for this novel so to speak. I could have clicked the publish button on KDP months earlier, but I just couldn't bring myself to do it right away. I know that my work is flawed; I'm not the next big name in the fantasy writing scene, and I likely never will be. I'm just some random kid who wants to try and make something of himself. I fully accept this reality, but that hasn't made coping with it easy.

When I started writing *"The Witch and The Wanderer,"* on Christmas night of 2020, I did so as an experiment. I was 19 years old at the time and had spent the entirety of my grade school years mostly avoiding my passion for writing because of this general fear of commitment I have. If I never try, then I can never fail, right? Wrong. So, on that night, I told myself that the quality of my work wasn't important; that the only thing that mattered was finishing my novel, simply so that I could find out if I was even capable of doing such. And well, it looks like that's exactly what ended up happening. I tried my best, and this book is the result. I don't think I'll ever be proud of the quality of the work I've here, but I am quite proud that I finished it.

Because the fact that this book is real, and has my name on it, is proof that I have what it takes to persevere in the writing business, and that while I'm not very good now, if I keep working hard, I may one day be great. If you've somehow made it this far, then thank you for helping me get an honest idea of just who exactly I want to be.

Made in the USA
Monee, IL
14 April 2022

94763517R00159